The Magic of Wynghorran Castle

By

Thomas Weal

The Magic of Wynghorran Castle
by
Thomas Weal

2nd Edition

ISBN No 978-0-9565559-0-8

Published by Wynghorran Enterprises

email: thomasweal@gmail.com

To Susan a special bear

Thanks to Dee Von Ell for the illustrations

CONTENTS

Grand Master Winkington 3rd

Chapter One CHANGE

The World of Bears had been in existence from the beginning of time, fitting in with the Universe as it was evolving; other worlds, other spirits all growing. There was no unrest, to the contrary there was harmony in the Universe. For centuries the Grand Masters of Bears, in line with all other powers, were settling into the modern world of man. In the time of Grand Master Winkington 3rd Wynghorran Castle was built by the bears under the guidance of the most senior architect and renowned stone mason Bear Lexington.

Today the three senior bears; Grand Master, Major Montgomery known as Bearmont and the Lord High Bear: William, Keeper of Spells stood in silence. Nothing was said, each bear was in a depth of thought that allowed exchange without words. One could feel the coldness in the air.

"To the Spell-room," commanded Winkington.

In a corner of the vast library they stood around the crystal table, the three bears who would shape the future of Bear World with the help of the Trusted Bears, the castle bears and the adoption bears living at the castle and their great friend Rugle the Dreaded Dragon. These three exuded an aura of total dedication to the challenge ahead. The destiny of the magic of Bear World was in their hands and they recognised and accepted the task ahead. For the first time in its magical history the castle had taken up the position of war against the unknown threat.

Building the castle

Bear Lexington completed the castle on time with the aid of the earliest bears. The bears had gathered from across the universes. Most of the bears had long journeyed the worlds but had never had a place of their own. Bear Lexington had worked with the Egyptian bears, the great Egyptian architects and the stone masons in the design and building of the pyramids. Lexington learnt, admired and absorbed their skills. His original plans for a home for the bears were based on the pyramid concept. He reasoned the pyramid style would give the bears protection for the future if the universe did ever come under threat. After long deliberation with the Grand Master and William it was decided that a home based on a castle would give most protection as well as a resting place for all bears waiting for their next lives. There are many stories to enthral, later in our tale, about the building of the castle. As the rooms were designed and built, the bears made ready the cathedral high library. This was the heart of their domain, the store for bear magic, for spells, for the history of Bear World. The massive, ancient tomes explained bear duties and the laws all bears must obey. During the building, the daily work of the Trusted Bears to help the born bears and their owners had to continue.

The bears moved in and over the next 1001 years established the castle developing all the rooms and the Great Hall. The west wing, used to house the teddy bears waiting for adoption was built with extra loving care. Dormitories were stacked with feather soft beds. Toffee scented windows played sunshine through the panes, into lounges overflowing with sofas stuffed with huggable loved fur from moulting elder bears. The newly fashioned caves sang with the music of water, tumbling along the sticky sugar rocks that lined the floor of the caverns. Here bears could sleep, play, swim or fish, recuperating from their duties in peoples' world. The great cave for Rugle the Dreaded Dragon was the deepest, warmest cave that ran out to the sea.

The west wing kitchen was legendary in bear world, mammoth in size, the cooking range stood twenty metres high and fifty metres long. Vast vats of porridge simmered constantly for any bear to help himself. Fish, fresh from the sea below, was prepared and cooked here. Berries, heavy with juice were eaten or stored and made into jams, quinces and jellies. The honey gathered from the hives was rich, soft and occasionally lavender scented – a very special treat. Orchards and the path to the forest led directly from the west wing. Here all bears gambolled, sun-bathed, played hide and seek, held picnics and told tales of their adventures in people world. The most enjoyable hours were when Aiggrowgar, the first of the Trusted Bears would tell stories of the old times: of battles fought, of heroic warrior bears who had gone before and of the many jokes he had played on long, resigned comrades. These were the best of times in Bear World.

Now the world was changing and the bears work grew as the demand for bear magic and bear comforting grew. Wars began across the universe, the harmony had gone. The land and seas of earth were engulfed in battles as the new elements came into being: greed, hate, jealousy, envy and revenge. Love and caring had to share with these new unwanted elements and the unthinkable became thought, that these intruders might take over from love and caring.

The bears work grew and they had to fight hard in order to hold the balance and try to win back time and peace from the unkind elements. The Grand Master, Winkington 3rd and the older bears had tried to find the source and the reasons for the unkind elements gaining power over earth, but as the influence grew the answer floated further away. The Lord High Bear, William, spent much time in the Spell-room of the library. William searched the ancient books for any clues. He also searched with the camera obscura looking out into the world in an effort to find a link between the good and the bad, but with no success.

The Grand Master called a meeting with William and the Major, the military guardian of the castle. William was troubled. He told the meeting that when he was searching for a reason into the growth of the new elements, he could sense a physical resistance, a direct block towards his search.

"I can't explain," said William, "but it feels real. It feels large and powerful, it is fighting me in a spiritual way. I am concerned for our safety and yet I cannot explain or define it, I'm sorry."

“No need,” replied the Grand Master, “I have felt the same threat but like you I am not sure just how real it is. My deeper thoughts when in meditation on these matters are not clear anymore. There is a cloud, as if I am being warned or threatened; it is a cold, unkind, corrosive presence. Whatever it is, it is not going to go away.”

Bearmont, although he did not acknowledge it, had also felt this presence in and above his beloved castle. He rubbed his white paws together and spoke in his soft growl.

“I will walk the castle – corridors, caverns, rooms and parapets bearing in mind what’s been said and discover if the castle will speak to me. This is the way I get my knowledge and inspiration. I will report back at first sun on morrowmarch.” Bearmont bowed with the merest hint of a nod, turned and with a back wave of his paw, strode swiftly across the marble floor. The other two bears looked at each other knowing that all bears work in different wondrous ways.

It happened on the morrowmarch, but well after the middle dayling, suddenly the sun shrank from view, a hazy, darkening film covering its brightness. It became cold, colder than night, colder than winter, a cold they had only heard about from distant cousins, the Polar bears. Something was wrong. The Grand Master, Winkington 3rd was fearful. He knew that something was about to threaten Bear World.

Winkington called as many as could gather to the Great Hall. William and Bearmont stood at his side.

"I have gathered you here," he explained, "to tell you of my concern. Our world is troubled by a presence that we cannot identify, nor yet can we see. I do not know what the threat is but I know there is one."

The Grand Master rose to his full height, his fur stood alert, bristling, his voice was grave and rumbling.

"We bears are, from this moment, at war with a force that I do not understand. The High Lord, Bearmont and I have been aware that of late something feels wrong and we are seeking a way to protect the castle and all bears. We believe the force, whatever it is, is trying to destroy our world of bears and the duties that we have to people; the goodness that we have always cherished, the love that we have embodied in the work that we do and the support that we give to all the bears in all the world. Without us, teddy bears could not meet the help requested by their owners, child or adult; boy or girl; black or white; pink or brown; of faith or not; it matters not in the magic world of bears."

Winkington paused. He moved two steps towards the gathered bears. His wise eyes glanced along the rows of now silent bears. His large heart shuddered within his giant chest and the great sorrow swept from his extended paws, encompassing all the bears present. They felt the warm sorrow and were afraid. Winkington smiled upon the trembling mass. His voice soared, way beyond the vast space of the library, it echoed along the corridors, it resounded through the walls, it reached the deepest caves and the highest turrets. That day Winkington's voice comforted, giving hope and motivation to every bear that was honoured to be in the Great Hall on that momentous day.

"Fear not my cubs. Our world is born of love, togetherness and service. I know not why in all the worlds we would be in danger, nor from whom or for what reason. This we will endeavour to find out. We will keep you informed. Be advised that we will need the assistance of you all. Some of you have military skills and will be guided and work alongside Bearmont."

The Major moved forward and stood beside the Grand Master, knowing that to be his place.

Winkington nodded at Bearmont and continued. "Some of you are academics, you will assist The Keeper of Spells. You will help his research into this new presence."

William moved to the other side of the Grand Master. The three senior bears together were formidable and the hearts of the bears were gladdened and strengthened. Winkington ordered the bears to stay together, to stay close in the Great Hall.

"By staying together our group spirit will protect us for a while until we can decide what we need to do to fight off this threat and protect our castle and Bear World."

It was at this moment that Winkington swivelled his great head towards William and then Bearmont and commanded, "To the Spell-room."

The Plan

Once again the three bears stood before the crystal table, they struck a similar pose, legs astride, paws behind their backs. Bearmont had walked the castle and was the first to speak,

"Comrades, I have walked the castle, its corridors and halls, its dungeons and turrets, she is silent to me, deadly silent. Is it possible for a castle to be scared?"

Winkington pondered, his furrow wrinkled as he raised his head to look at Bearmont. He spoke slowly his voice only one word in front of his thoughts.

"As we all know, our castle is made of stone. Stone carved and placed by the hand of Lexington our master builder and in those stones is woven his love and caring. He learnt the skills and knowledge of the Egyptian pyramids and I am sure there is something of that imbued within the castle. So Bearmont my friend, yes, I believe that our castle has detected the danger and could well be scared as you put it. I suggest that you have words with Lexington and ask him if he is able to detect any feelings of ill in the castle and maybe between you, you can get to understand how the castle is feeling. We must, at all costs, protect the castle and those within its walls."

"And how do we do that?" Bearmont broke in. "We do not have guns or cannons and we can't yet see our enemy."

The Grand Master turned towards Bearmont. "Enemy? What enemy? We do not yet know if this is an enemy. We only know something is a threat, a grave threat - that I do believe, but choose your words with care Bearmont. We do not wish to alarm our teddy bears more than is necessary. As I have said to them we will require their assistance with military and academic endeavours, but as yet we do not need to bear the walls with lookouts."

Winkington allowed himself a smile at this thought. The brave rag-bag assortment of adoption bears; old ones, young ones, patched up ones, tired ones rejuvenated by their stay at the castle, small or large, curly fur or loved away bare bears, all would be enthusiastic in their help and would eagerly follow his orders. His thoughts returned to the present task.

"Our power of thought must be used at this moment to hold the threat at bay. This can be done best by all the bears, collectively protecting the castle from within. Together we have strength. Keeping the threat at bay will give us time to understand and decide how to fight back."

Bearmont responded, "Wise words Grand Master. We will prepare for battle and base that preparation on the knowledge we have."

"But we have very little knowledge as of yet," said William, with a large frown on his small face.

Bearmont continued, "But we do, we have more than you realise. Do you agree that the castle will be the battlefield?"

The other two nodded. "We know that it's not going to be troops storming the ramparts." More nods.

"We know that we cannot see what form the threat will take." Again two bear heads nodded. Bearmont rubbed his grizzled chin with the back of his paw and spoke again, slowly, every word weighing heavily on his mind.

"This battle will be won by mental rightness. It will be you William who'll guide us through this. It is a battle of magic. I believe the many spells, the learning, the lessons we have gathered over time were all for this."

His muscled hairy arm swept in an arc encompassing the library, "And it is all in this room. My task in this is to protect and support you both in any way I can. Nothing else, just keep you Grand

Master and you Lord High Bear safe, together with the other bears and our home, safe from whatever is coming our way. That is my duty as guardian of the castle and a duty I will perform to my best ability."

Bearmont clicked his feet together and saluted the two bears who had gravely listened to his small speech.

"As always Major, your instincts guide us well." Winkington swivelled, looking from one companion to the other. "We three will triumph, with the aid of the Trusted Bears, the adoption and castle bears and our great friend Rugle we will succeed. Let us return to the teddy bears in the Great Hall and tell them of our plans."

Winkington marched from the library, shoulders back, his fur raised and straight, his solid bearprints thumping the floor. The two bears following needed extra bearprints as they could not match the Grand Master's long stride.

Wynghorran Castle

Chapter 2 THE LIGHT

The unexpected happened following the cold chill that had fallen over the castle. The next dawn was bright sunshine but not from a blue sky, but a black sky. It was a column of sunshine, a bright light that at first mimicked a summer's day. By middling-day it became apparent that it was a pillar of light that did not move round as did the sun, but stationed itself above the castle, its white light engulfing the courtyard and part of the terrace. On this primary day it emitted no heat, just a shimmering light that undulated on its journey from the sky to the earth.

The three great bears had gathered in Winkington's private domain. The gargantuan room housed the Grand Master's personal possessions. His chain of office, suspended from entwined vines, glistened in the light, burnished by the long presence of his fur rubbing the gold. His ceremonial robes were draped across the four metre width of the stag antlers. The honeycomb bookcase displayed books that told of the succession of Masters and spoke of the laws and duties of Bear World. Above the high fire-place was the most treasured of items, Bear World's coat of arms with the motto 'Servo Veneflicus' (Keep the Magic).

Winkington shifted his gaze upon the Major,

"Tell me Bearmont, I know that you have ventured outside to view the light. Do you have any ideas of what we might be up against?"

"No," answered Bearmont, "it was just a very unfriendly presence. The air was warm like sunshine but the warmth was disturbing. I wasn't able to stay outside for more than a twelfth of time, but what I did notice was the bushes in the garden. Their leaves have turned golden, by the morrowmarch I fear they will be crisped and dead".

Winkington drew his giant arms from behind his broad back and spread his paws flat on the grape-encrusted surface of the diamond shaped table. William and Bearmont glanced at each other, as they waited silent for the Grand Master to speak. The bear's warm heavy breath was the only soft noise within the room. The breathing melodious in its trio of sound.

"William, have you learned anything from the library scrolls, or books or ancient documents?"

"Nothing specific," replied William. "Except that I am drawn to the oldest section, the Egyptian manuscripts gathered at the beginning of the 1001 years of building. But at least this gives me an area in which to look. I believe the castle is guiding me."

Winkington nodded, "Good, good. Go with your instincts, they are well honed over many aeons. Trust them my faithful friend, on just such things does Bear World now depend."

The Grand Master stood straight and moved backwards from the table. He turned towards one apple-scented window that looked into the grounds. The window reflected the light beam that was illuminating the terrace.

"This beam of light," Winkington began, "where does it come from? Light travels at about 300,000 kilometres per second. So does it come from the stars or is it a manifestation begun just from the sky to the castle? This is also more than just light," he paused, then continued, "think of it as an upside–down custard tart, with the custard just waiting to fall out onto the castle. Neither is this just ordinary custard for it is flavoured with unique substances and elements."

Winkington glanced over his shoulder at the two bears and took note of their incredulous stares. He sighed and faced his friends.

"Please bears do not ask me to explain for I cannot."

William and Bearmont had not been surprised by Winkington's analogy, for all bears gave examples in terms of food; that was their heritage. No, what had startled them was Winkington's belief that something could possible spray out from the light and engulf the castle.

The three bears stood silent for a few micro's before the Grand Master, slowly and with care, spoke again.

"Bears, let us ponder our own thoughts and look at the light in our own way, for the remainder of the dayling. William you might want to engage with Beggrowgar and I'm sure that Aiggrowgar will join forces with you Bearmont. Let us meet at this table middle of the morrowmarch. As for me I will climb down to the cave and talk to Rugle."

As he ambled away Winkington spoke quietly, more to himself than the others. "Hmm, more like a playful puppy than a dreadful dragon!"

William and Bearmont called the five Trusted Bears together. As next in the chain of command and responsibility they needed to be informed in more detail than had been given to the teddy bears in the Great Hall. Beggrowgar, the inquisitive one, asked the first question.

"But what does it mean? Surely light cannot hurt us, why is the Grand Master so concerned?" Beggrowgar knew deep down that there must be a threat, of that he doubted not. If Winkington was concerned then there was reason for them all to be concerned, but what was this specific danger? He and the other Trusted Bears needed a much better understanding if they were to be of good aid and help reassure the adoption bears.

William smiled at his designate with a fondness born of long years trying to answer his friend's never ending questions. William knew he had chosen his designate wisely. Beggrowgar would never slake his thirst for knowledge; the library, the Spell-room and its magic would forever be safe in his paws.

"As you all know, we have centuries of books and spells available to us. Over quarts of time I have studied, read, browsed and glanced throughout. My favourites are well-pawed," William laughed and then continued with his explanation.

"I know what books we have and there are a number that refer to light. Light comes in so many forms and shades. There is a dark light, dark light is so bright that it reflects into itself and is hidden from vision by eating itself. One cannot see it but it distorts, engulfs and is very dangerous. Sunshine light is coloured, colours that make the rainbow. The different colours have different powers and different species can see different bands of colours. Light travels at extreme speed and as a general rule does not harm when it arrives at solid mass, but look directly when it arrives on you and it will injure your eyes. A flash of light can frighten and cause blindness for a few seconds or even permanently. The adoption bears well know how much comfort is needed by their younger owners when these flashes light the sky at night. There is also a concentrated beam called a laser that can cut through fur, wood, metal and stone, so you see Beggrowgar light in the wrong paws and used as a means of destruction is deadly and therefore a cause for concern."

The five bears had listened silently to this explanation, honoured to be sharing William's great knowledge. But they were troubled and ill at ease, now understanding their Grand Master's concern and very real fear for the safety of the castle and the bears within. As with other moments of tension it was Aiggrowgar who lightened the mood.

"So, not just a case of covering up the old fur or taking shade in the dungeons then," he laughed.

"Unfortunately not," replied William, "in my opinion, if we do nothing the light will eventually crumble the castle down around us."

"At least we'll have custard to go with the crumble," bellowed Bearmont.

At this they all laughed until tears sprinkled down their fur and two of them fell with the mirth and rolled higgley-piggley across the lawned floor, but their friendship and shared humour strengthened them for the difficult morrows to come.

Chapter 3 RUGLE THE DREADED DRAGON

Rugle had heard Winkington climbing down to the cave and had skipped out to the entrance to greet his old friend. He waited impatiently as the big bear approached. Rugle loved the moments he spent on the shore talking to all of the senior bears, but he loved the Grand Master most of all. Their deep friendship and mutual respect was founded on the plenteous years of discussion, tales, escapades and sharing fish together. They had in the earliest times recognised the unique solitariness of their roles for there were no others as they. They both bore heavy burdens for a myriad of reasons. Their lives were incomparable, for Rugle's had been based on bringing joy and magic to small children in the fantasy times. Winkington's had always been based on servitude and the vast responsibility of being the Grand Master. On his massive shoulders rested the continuance of Bear World. In their oneness they had sought each other's company to share secrets, doubts and troubled times. Only to each other could they admit fear and that awful sense of just once in a quantum not knowing what to do.

This dayling Rugle had seen the beam of light appear over the castle and he was excited. He imagined this was something the bears had arranged and he was intrigued to know what purpose it might serve and what fun might be had from this pillar of sunshine. He was, therefore, perplexed to see that Winkington was walking heavily along the sand, his head bowed in thought, his arms hung motionless at his sides. This was not a good sight.

"My friend I am delighted to see you, come share my rock and tell me your news," smiled Rugle. Up close he could now see Winkington's grey eyes looked dull and his mouth firm.

"You look of heavy heart Old Bear, what troubles you?" One of Rugle's long ears uncurled to touch his friend's shoulder in a comforting mode.

The large, long, deep sigh that broke forth from Winkington explained more of his troubled mind than did the next twelfth time of detailed story. Listening in silence while Winkington spoke, Rugle had been motionless. Now he stirred, rose to his full height and thundered to the sand from the rock upon which both had sat.

"We will eat first, strength must always be fed, without it we cannot function, act or plan."

Two strides took the dragon deep into the sea, his hooked red-nailed toes flashed from the water spiked with an abundance of conger eel. With one flame throw from his open mouth the eel was skinned, cooked, quartered and served to Winkington cradled upon the perimeter of Rugle's wing. The shared meal was enjoyed with litres of mead, gigantic burps and a conviviality that is spontaneous when friends meet.

"To return to the task, of what would you ask of me Old Bear?" Rugle said as his rolled, black tongue licked around the length of his mouth.

"It would be helpful to know from where the light emanates," began Winkington, "is it from the stars, from space, or is its origin just from the sky? If we can identify the source, then maybe we will begin to understand what it is and more importantly, what it might become."

"That should not be a problem, I will fly to as near the top as I can. This is not such a bad dayling as I began to believe. An adventure to get my wings into, haarhha haarhha haarhha!"

The grimbled dragon watched as the Grand Master strode back along the sand. His shoulders had lifted and his fur was more bristled. The dragon knew that once more their friendship had lightened the load a few micros for the one carrying the burden and he was warmed by this knowledge. He was also excited at the prospect of the adventure ahead, his desire to fly was great but in this time often without purpose. Now he had reason and he once again, in his paired hearts, thanked the worlds for bringing the bears to his island. That had been the magical day.

Rugle the Dreaded Dragon had lived by the sea since time immemorial. His small cave was warm but damp and dark. He was the last of his line and the loneliness bowed his head and weighed heavily on his wings. His role long forgotten by man-world.

Rugle loved the large hump-shaped rock that jutted from the fore-shore, as if a giant hand had pushed it into the sand and then abandoned it. He would curl up around the rock resting his long neck on the curving top and gaze at the ever-changing sea. His scales would lift for the warming rays of sun to enter deep into his body. This was the fuel for his fire. Not that he needed fire nowadays; there were no adversaries, no monsters, no pirates to disturb his long, solitary days.

The magic time had arrived when Rugle, in his usual place refuelling, saw on the far distant horizon a small dark speck. His long neck snaked upwards, his curled eyelashes half closing sheltering his eyes for a better view. He watched transfixed as the dark speck grew ever larger, ever forwards, tacking across the sea. The speck morphed into a shape with sails thrust upwards, billowing red, harnessing the wind. When just two leagues distant Rugle, now standing on his heavy 4m hind-legs, could see a bear before the sail.

Rugle's metre length ears uncurled to catch on the wind the cry -

"20 degrees N by N.W my salties." The boat sailed into Rugle's small golden bay. This was to be his introduction to Bear World.

The Flight

Flapping and circling in massive arcs upon the sand, Rugle stretched and splayed his wings. Webbed across a quintet of bony spokes on either side of his shoulder blades, the wings were spectacular. They dwarfed his giant body, taking 5/8ths of his mass. The dragon could easily fly at middle-mast, but this dayling he had need of the full power the wings could command. He might need to go nearer the stars than ever before. The shimmering, fluorescent limes, lemons and tinges of red that outlined the curving edges glinted and reflected in the sea beyond.

The castle had stilled, all within was quiet and although Winkington had not ordered the bears to keep a look-out from the ramparts when the light had arrived, that was precisely what every bear in the kingdom was now doing. Standing from every vantage point they could find, hanging from gables, climbing the turrets, crowding the windows, each and every bear wanted to watch the brave Rugle take flight. Of course they could have easily stood along the shore-line and been as near as to feel his hot breath as he gasped in mammoth clouds of air to sustain his flight.........BUT even a bear is wary when the Dreaded Dragon starts his flight run and prudence, as some had costly learnt, was a virtue.

Rugle snorted thrice, flapped in unison the giant wings once more and gathered speed as he lollopped across the ground. His 4m hind legs covered acres of sand and as he reached the peninsular with its jagged rocks reaching up to the castle, he soared skywards. As he circled the castle Rugle could see the many arms of the bears waving their paws excitedly and on the wind he caught the sound of their cheering and clapping. Rugle knew the magnificent sight he created in flight and his chest billowed with pride. Just for one micro he yearned for the old familiar feel of having, once again, a small boy riding his back, but that would be play and this was work.

The dragon flew fourfold leagues upwards and away from the light, he wanted to see if the source could be viewed from afar. From his height Rugle could see that indeed the light was a straight column that appeared to be a slowly rotating solid shape. Round as a pillar and of equal breadth throughout its entirety. It was simple to see that the end touching the earth did not move its perimeter. The light was stationary except for the revolving movement. It was like a giant corkscrew without the indentations. The light shimmered as it turned, yellow at its core fading to a luminescent white towards the outside. Rugle could not discern whether the twisting revolved upwards or downwards or simply circled. The whole thing was an enigma. Rugle hovered, the giant wings lazily turning in figures of eight to keep him held in the darkened sky. Suddenly he shot aloft; legs held straight beneath him, wings folded back, neck arrowed. The gasp of breath that propelled him would last a thrice of time. Upwards, upwards, upwards, the earth below took on the sight not of trees or buildings or even towns, but countries and oceans. Still Rugle rocketed until the earth curved and the only air was contained within his labyrinth of lungs. Turning horizontally Rugle circumnavigated the column, it must have been a furlong thick, but of the top there was no sign. It stretched above, lost towards the stars. There was unease in watching it. This was a new sensation for the dragon and it perplexed him. Why should it be so? Did the lack of heat emanating from the light make him troubled? A cold light was indeed a new phenomenon, but why did it feel a threat?

Perhaps I am being influenced by what the Grand Master has already imparted to me about the beam, he thought. But, very soon Rugle was to know that the threat was real. Real and extremely dangerous to him.

As he could not find the birth of the light, Rugle decided to descend, still navigating his way around the pillar to check for any differences or changes along its length. The light dazzled and realising he would soon need to gather fresh air, Rugle's concentration had shifted and he failed to compensate for the narrowing circles he was making on his descent. His wing tips had become within a stride of the light and the near part began to glow and pulsate. Rugle felt a sharp pull on his scales and without his command his scales lifted instantaneously. A rush of heat exited from his body and was engulfed into the light. Alarmed and now alert the dragon realised the light was feeding from him. It wanted his warmth, his fire. It would suck his fuel from him, leaving him empty, undefended and alone in the vast sky. He struggled to break away, his muscled legs thrust forward as if they could dig into a non-existent ground and halt the pull on his body. The gigantic wings windmilled, back pedalling to stop Rugle's advance into the light. He needed more air but none was forthcoming at this height. Self-preservation automatically took over and with a mighty roar and the last of his air Rugle threw a red-flame of breath at the light. The effort propelled him backwards out of the light's gravity and he started to drop. Energy and air gone Rugle was as a stone racing towards Earth. The wings stretched bat-like, hindering his gathering speed and twisting mid-stream Rugle watched the earth rush upwards towards him.

The Grand Master, William and Bearmont had waited outside during the dragon's flight. They had positioned themselves around his humped rock, their backs resting against the smooth stone. Hearing the rush of air above them they scrambled on all fours swiftly along the fore-shore, their paws leaving deep indentations on the damp beach. Only just out of harm they turned simultaneously and saw their great friend crash in a billowing cloud of sand upon the ground. The shuddering crunch shook the castle, apples fell from trees, the bees took flight, porridge spilt from the great vats and rocks tumbled into the restless waves. Rugle's fall was of earthquake proportions. The three bears had been knocked to the ground by the shock-wave but once more they scrambled to their feet and once again on all fours now rushed in the opposite direction back towards the non-moving dragon.

<u>The Old Times</u>

Long before Rugle had become the last of his kind and solitary on the island he had lived his life with adventure, excitement, fun and the company of a host of small children. He, like many creatures, had been appointed to be companion, mentor, confidant, playmate and comforter to any child who called upon his services. Not all children called and of those who did mostly all were boys. In these earlier times there had been creatures sufficient to attach to every needy child. A friend of their own for as long as was wanted. A friend who could be at one's side in the blink of an eye or, who could hide away patiently waiting until called upon once more. These were the fine times when magic and imagination were all. Times to savour, times to remember, times to recall and share.

Rugle remembered all his children, some more favourably than others, but he had loved them all. The periods between were also good – as long as not too long, for boredom and too much sitting was as bad for a dragon's waistline as for a bears. Tom was to be Rugle's last child-hood friend, although this knowledge was thankfully unknown to him until the end. Tom was brave, lonely, red-haired and eight years old and he lived on the top floor of a very high building. This was where he first met Rugle, up on the roof where Tom was not allowed to go.

"Hello Dragon," shouted Tom as he spotted Rugle sitting between the chimney pots, "how are you today?"

Rugle had been asleep in his cave when he first heard the 'hello' but, as said, in the blink of Tom's eyelashes Rugle was lazing on the roof.

"I am very well, thank you Tom," replied the dragon, "I am just sitting here enjoying the sun's rays on my back."

"Good, let's go then, I have to be at the top of the mountain by 2.30 today," said Tom in the matter of fact way that boy's speak to dragons at their first meet. He easily climbed between Rugle's shoulder blades and holding on to the grimbled elongated neck, they were away into the clouds, over oceans, and up onto the high mountain well before 2.30pm.

Tom glanced around, "I thought there would be snow up here........" Before the sentence had been completed gentle tumble-flakes of snow fell covering the ground more quickly than could ever be done in towns.

"Thought there would be." Tom cried "Come on Rugle lets play."

The snowman was as big as one of Rugle's hind-legs. The hat, scarf, carrot nose and plum eyes were easily found behind bushes and shrubs by Tom..... once Rugle knew for what the boy searched. Snow-ball fights, sledge rides, slides down the dragon's frosty tail and even rein-deer, with their soft, velvet moist noses, were all embraced that first afternoon. Tom stopped, turned his head and listened.

"That's my mum calling me for tea, better go, see you tomorrow Dragon." Tom skipped a few steps along the mountain plateau went through the door on the roof and jumped two by two down the stairs to his flat.

Rugle returned to his cave, exhilarated with the afternoon's adventure and his new friend. The fine times were beginning anew.

Rugle and Tom's fine times were a delight and a source of wonderment to both. They lasted for the length of time that Tom's imagination could remain in the childhood realm that allows play beyond the boundaries of time and space and the need for companions of one's own kind.

Mountains were a favourite of Tom's and the roof was always a good launching pad. It involved avoiding the sheets hung out to dry along the spaces between chimney pots. But with Tom in command Rugle could fly straight up, or launch horizontally, hopping from roof-top to roof-top far above the bustling city below, whose people never looked aloft to see the magic taking place in the skies. Sometimes the boy wanted Rugle to dive down, darting and twisting around the tall buildings, whooshing past office windows, where adults sat in rows gazing at the glowing screens, never ever lifting their heads to see the small laughing boy riding by on the back of the fiercest, most enormous, most magnificent, most awesome dragon whoever had lived.

Together Rugle and Tom adventured to the stars, exploring worlds where the sun was purple and the seas ice-cream. Giant ships travelled these oceans with fierce pirates burying treasure beneath chocolate shores. Tom, with Rugle's help, always defeated the pirates, captured the treasure and as they rode away Tom would cry,

"Sink the ship, Rugle." Rugle with one gigantic roar of flame would melt the ice-cream sea and the defeated vessel would sink into the soggy mess.

On Tom's way home they would pass mile long space-ships cruising to far galaxies. Once he even gave a lift to a passing space-man who had stayed outside of his ship too long. Tom invited him home for tea, but his mum didn't believe him and left the hungry space-man on the roof with Rugle till bed-time.

Often in the early times, Tom would call Rugle to play with him at home. The dragon would hide in the fridge, or beneath Tom's bed. Once Tom even found him asleep with the cat, curled up together in the old wicker basket. Tom was always good at finding the numerous hiding places one could squeeze a dragon into. His mum was useless; she could never spot him, even if Rugle stared straight at her. Tom never queried Rugle's changing size, he knew in the logical way of small boys that dragons fitted whatever place they were in. He was always the 'just right' size to snuggle against Tom in bed. The dragon could be a cuddle size when Tom wanted to hold him in his arms, this was really important when his mum and dad argued and the angry words would intrude into the small bedroom of the softly crying child. Rugle's wings could then wrap around Tom and his sobs would quieten and his fears would go.

A favourite place to explore was beneath the sea. Rugle's giant feet would swim them to the depths of oceans. Sting rays came to play, but sharks avoided Rugle's dangerous wings. Corals were for hopping along and Tom learnt that the sea-weed forests were the nurseries for the tiny sea-horses who were baby dragons. Dragons waiting to grow lungs and wings and emerge chrysalis-like from the green sea. Sometimes they would even ride rainbows, sliding down the magical colours and landing by the pot of gold. Tom was not interested in trying to carry these pots home for he feared his mother would ask too many questions, but he always thought it was a shame that he could not surprise her.

One day Tom wanted to take Rugle to school, but as usual the boy's mother was in a hurry and now they were all late. It really wasn't Tom's fault that they were delayed because he had first tried to get Rugle into his school bag. His mum had told him not to be so silly and so Rugle was now walking behind them, keenly watching the other children already sitting on the school bus. Tom's mum pushed him on the bus with a big shove to his back.

"Enough of this nonsense now get off to school and don't lose your P.E. kit today."

The bus doors shut behind him but as Tom turned to sit down he could see Rugle still standing at the stop next to his mother. Tom frantically beat on the doors of the bus and wailed to the driver,

"Stop, stop, please stop. You have left my friend behind. Go back, go back, he'll be lost he doesn't know where to go."

Within a few yards of the bus stop Tom's hysterical cries made the driver stop and look back. The man thought he must have left a child behind, but he could only see a few parents still waiting for the bus to disappear from sight.

"What's the matter young fella, no need to get so frightened. Calm down, there is only your mum there."

"Let me off, you must let me off, now NOW." Tom's voice rose in anguish again and the puzzled and now slightly annoyed driver reversed the bus and opened the doors. Tom fell off the bus onto his knees in his panic to reach Rugle.

"Whatever is the matter," cried his mother as she held open her arms for Tom to rush into. The woman thought something dreadful must have happened. Tom rushed passed his mother and flung his arms wide around the dragon.

"You didn't let Rugle get on the bus; you made him get left behind," Tom accused.

His mother, now relieved, angry and embarrassed all at the same time grabbed Tom by the shoulder, swung her left arm high in the air and smacked the back of Tom's legs hard. Immediately regretting this act of violence in front of other mothers, she pulled Tom along the road not stopping until they reached their own front door.

"Just wait until I tell your father about this, I've never been so ashamed in all my life. We will not have any more nonsense about this dragon of yours ever again. I never want to hear you talk of him again. Understand?"

Tom had not heard any of his mother's threats, the smack had hardly even registered through the thickness of his trousers and long jacket. No, Tom was just so happy to be sent up to his bedroom where he and Rugle, his best friend, would be able to play for the rest of the day.

Once the driver had seen Tom was safely with his mother he put the bus in gear and started again on the short journey to the school. Felicity, who was the same age as Tom, had been sitting opposite the door of the bus and had therefore had a front row seat of the entire fracas, she now turned to the older boy next to her and said solemnly,

"Tom is so silly, Mrs. McEvoy doesn't let dragons come into class."

On The Beach

It took a quadful of daylings to mend the broken dragon. Under Winkington's view the bears tended to their hurting friend. Unable to move him they cared for him where he lay on the soft sand.

William sought out the strongest healing incantation from the Spell-room. He had paced, agitated, amongst row upon row of the library book-shelves. His knowledge, although not beaten, was unaccustomed to finding spells for other than bears. At last William decided and he galloped to the beach, there sitting upon the dragon's crown he intoned with soothing voice into each mangled ear. Thrice dayling did The Lord High: Keeper of Spells perform this restoring ritual.

Duggrowsar, the fourth Trusted Bear, patched the torn, ripped wings with honey balm and spiders thread gathered fresh before the dew could dry the silken weave. From her medicines, learnt and practiced in the times of the Chinese dynasties, she selected, mixed and pounded herbs and seeds and, soft as a whisper, applied the poultices on the purple raised high bruises.

The other Trusted Bears paired to see-saw the great bellows they had dragged, pushed and heaved across the rocks and sand. Non-stop they breathed for the silent dragon, allowing colossal puffs of air to enter the flared nostrils. The rhythmic pounding of their massive padded feet worked the bellows and in unison matched the feeble beats of the great beast's paired hearts. Gradually, imperceptibly, the duo of beats strengthened, quickened and could be seen with the rising and falling of his enormous chest.

The adoption teddy bears heated the fallen one's brow with hot spiced water. They dipped their paws in sugared milk and squeezed the sweet, creamy drops from their sticky fur into his sagging mouth. They lay against and on the battered body, stretching their arms wide to coat the dragon with their warm insulating fur so to refuel him. As their ally shifted and heaved, uncomfortable with pain, the living fur blanket undulated and mirrored his shuddering contours.

From night-dark to night-grey Bearmont stood fourfold afront the sleeping dragon guarding him from the noises and movements that sound within the dark of night. Methodically at ninth of the cycle, he lit the flaming beacons that outlined and cast shadows around the sleeping dragon.

In this way the Grand Master orchestrated the saving of his great friend Rugle the Dreaded Dragon.

Chapter 4 THE SEARCH

Beggrowgar had started working with Lord High Bear William when the library was built but still empty of the many books, scrolls and spells that needed to be catalogued, arranged and displayed in the grand surroundings of the vast chamber that had become the library. The collection, gathered over many aeons, had been carefully stored in trunks and wrapped and protected with acid-free tissue paper interleaved to prevent any deterioration. Before the castle was built the treasured books had been kept in many places in small collections. In some instances just a few books and manuscripts had been entrusted to bears who lovingly kept, guarded and so preserved their heritage in the hope that one morrowmarch there would be a place for the collection to come together.

The dayling that the final consignment of books had arrived at the castle was marked with a celebration of feasting and fireworks that had illuminated the night-dark to dayling. Rugle had been given the task of lighting the fireworks and had done so with gentle fire breaths so controlled that the gathered bears had watched in awe.

The task of bringing the collection together and arranging the many sections had been of mammoth proportions. More than once had the task seemed impossible in its enormity. It was Beggrowgar who had encouraged, cajoled and made the task fun for all the adoption bears who had been drafted in to help. They had carried, unpacked, sorted, stacked, misplaced and found again the books needed from the tall piles covering the diamond patterned marquetry floor of the library. Beggrowgar enjoyed working closely with William and William was pleased to have under his guidance such an able bear who was willing to give the total dedication needed to make the new library successful. At the grand opening, in front of all the castle bears, William had announced, to rousing cheers and rollicking back-slapping that Beggrowgar would, from that day, be the Lord High Bear designate. During his brief acceptance speech the teddy bears gaped in wonderment as Beggrowgar grew thrice enths taller, such was his pride at the honour bestowed upon him.

Beggrowgar was a new bear compared to some of the older Trusted Bears. He had first entered the world of books in Persia working alongside a Royal Trader who had a keen interest, academically and financially, in the selling, buying and collecting of books from all the old Empires. Books were traded and usually sold for very high values. All the old civilizations recognised that the information and knowledge books contain is of immense value. The existence and continuation of the old Empires was founded on knowledge and an understanding of history. The wise ones appreciated that knowledge is power, just as it is today. The velvet-furred bear's love of books deepened and developed over the long periods of time and he came to learn the immense value and joy of accumulating information just for its own sake.

Owing to the size of the great chamber that was the library and Spell-room William and Beggrowgar, for much of their time worked separately, meeting up at regular intervals to exchange and update each other on their findings. As the Grand Master had asked of them, they now met in the Spell-room, but a full quadmorrows later than expected. Both bears had been involved in the caring of Rugle following his dreadful accident and both were conscious of the urgency to find a solution to the threat from the light. During the time-healing of the dragon, the castle had been affected ever more greatly by the presence of the light pillar. The trees were now bare of leaves, the lawns were brown and crisp. The normal smell of warm sunshine and honey popcorn that greeted visitors to the library had now changed to one of burnt popcorn and the air was acrid and too warm.

The paired bears were aware that the answer, or even a key part of it, might not be in the library at all but if it was, they had to find it. Although they had only been aware of the threat for a short time each in his own way had scavenged the recesses of their knowledge for a sign or clue that would give them some insight, but nothing had come to either bear. Starting from opposite ends they had decided to walk the library; the corridors, the alcoves, the stair-cases and the Spell-room. William wanted to discern if they could feel any part of the library or a particular book reaching out to them. In the way that he found individual spells he wondered if they could narrow their search by fellowfeel. The walk had produced nothing new. Each bear took up position around the crystal table, standing square to each other with elbows on the table and paws clasped, they looked into each other's eyes. William spoke first.

"We have so many books, scrolls and artifacts from worlds far and near so what am I looking for I ask myself. Tell me faithful friend, if we put our minds together can we uncover or even recognise whatever it is we seek?"

The second bear smiled at his mentor and answered in a positive growl, "William you have never yet been unable to help us. Whether it be here in the castle, or a request from an adopted bear, or a particular spell, or even a query from that old rascal Aiggrowgar, who does like to test your knowledge, you always, always find something that answers the question or provides comfort. Why look how you have just helped save Rugle, without your incantations daily, the healing would have taken a lot longer even with Dooey's skill and the Grand Master's attentiveness."

The younger bear stopped, scratched his head and then placing both his paws over William's knarled bony paws he continued shyly. "As has already been said to you, go with your own instincts. Each time you come to the library you are drawn to the Egyptian section. Have you thought William that maybe you are drawn there not to find a particular book but because the answer may lie in Egypt itself?"

At this revelation William leapt into the air, thudded the table, making the pile of books that had stood upon it rain down upon the floor and bellowed, "By the Great Grizzly himself, dear, dear friend, you have hit upon something that should have been so obvious to me that I must be a panda not to have seen it. Of course you are right, that is what we must do, go to Egypt. At once, be quick, we must tell Winkington of your great idea. Now we have a plan."

Before he had finished talking William was on his way out of the library leaving Beggrowgar to scamper along behind trying to keep up.

The Grand Master finished listening to his very excited Lord High Bear. "We could go immediately Winkington, I can arrange for Eaggrowgar to mind the library while I am gone. He has experience of all the daily duties and can handle any queries most proficiently." exclaimed William as he paced to and fro enthusiastically.

Winkington smiled and let forth an almost inaudible sigh. He had strong, paternal feelings for all the senior bears and loved and welcomed their enthusiasm and commitment. He disliked having to curb any suggestions or actions they proposed, but it was his duty to make sure that everything and everybody worked as efficiently as possible and for the good of them all. The great bear bent forward and placed his paw on the little lilac bear's stooped shoulder.

"William, let us think for a micro on the best way to carry out this marvellous plan of yours." He turned his head towards Beggrowgar, "And well done to you BG for enlightening us with your wonderful idea." A second sigh escaped from the Grand Master, as his gaze turned once more towards William and he patted the teddy bear's shoulder thrice more.

"No-one is more valued than you for being able to operate the library and Spell-room. This is a grave time for Bear World and I do not know when I might be calling on your knowledge or even what help I might need from you old friend in the coming morrows. But, I am certain that I do need you by my side. The burden I now carry to ensure the safety of the castle and all within can only be lightened by the help of you and Bearmont. We trio must remain as one. William my great friend I understand your disappointment with my decision but I must keep you here at the castle with me."

At this pronouncement William slumped to the floor and rolled over onto his back. He growled deep within his chest and Beggrowgar, who had been standing a little to one side during the conversation, could feel the vibration through his padded feet. Slowly, the little bear stood on his hind feet and faced the Grand Master.

"I, of course, concur with your wish Grand Master. Yes, it is disappointing, but your reasoning is, as always, without fault. We trio must oversee what is happening and the castle is the best place from which we can command." William paused and looked as his designate. Beggrowgar's face gave no sign of how he had taken the news. "But please tell me Winkington, is it not a good idea to journey to Egypt to seek further information and perhaps the chance to find an answer?"

"Indeed, it is an excellent idea and one we must follow up, as you say, immediately. It is just that it cannot be you who goes," replied Winkington, eager to make sure that his friend did not feel that his plan was being dismissed.

"Then who?" queried William.

"As you know Lexington worked in Egypt centuries ago and has many contacts there. Coggrowgar has also travelled with him many times to distant shores. I would be very grateful William if you would talk to Lexington about everything you have discovered so far, tell him to what you are particularly drawn and if you have any feelings about where his travel should take him or to whom he should speak, that would help enormously. I need your help William, without your input Lexington cannot succeed. Go to him now and tell him of your plan."

The Grand Master watched as William, once more, purposefully strode from the room followed, as always by his designate. This time Winkington's sigh was of relief that he had managed to placate his close friend and also convey his gratitude, for he really did believe the trip to Egypt would be of immense value and add to their armour for the coming battle.

The Journey

Lexington left the castle with Coggrowgar on the long journey to the land of the pyramids and in particular to visit the Cairo Museum of Antiquities. It was here he would find his old friend Bear Toomey who was the bear to Syeed Mazoon, the curator of the Museum. Bear Toomey was a bear of many births who had travelled the length and breadth of the pyramid lands with Mazoon. Toomey had been the museum bear for many aeons and had served and learnt from numerous museum curators. He was a Trusted Bear who had always chosen to work in faraway hot lands disliking the cold of some places that aggravated his rheumatism.

Although a long journey in distance for Lexington and his companion, it was but a short journey in bear time. They hurried directly to the high office above the main centre hall of the museum. Bear Toomey was expecting them but was intrigued to know the reason for the visit. Long experience had taught him that bears did not make long journeys just for social visits. Bear World was much too busy a place for that. It was only adoption bears who had holidays between births. Dealing with human demands and requests, especially if their owners were children, meant the adopted teddy bears needed time to recuperate and socialise with their own kind.

Toomey's appearance belied the fact that he was a wise studious bear, as the oceans of time that he had spent in the sun showed on his worn and, in places, faded fur. Toomey had been in all the pyramids spread throughout the Egyptian desert and had learnt many of their secrets alongside the museum curators. His fascination never ceased when viewing for the very first time the vast array of objects that the kings had deemed necessary to store in their tombs. In the beginning time the treasures rescued were housed in the old museum that was comprised of nothing more than a collection of sheds and tents. Too many artefacts had been stolen by individuals and countries who plundered the wealth of the pharaohs, either to sell or for their own collections. The new museum was necessary and secure.

Toomey welcomed Lexington as the old friend he was and the two old comrades chatted joyfully.

Lexington stopped suddenly saying, "Sorry CG we got carried away."

Lexington introduced Coggrowgar to his friend and then settled down to explain what was happening at Wynghorran Castle and why they had travelled so far. He detailed what they knew about the light, the attack on Rugle the Dreaded Dragon and the horrendous consequences. Lexington outlined the thoughts of the Grand Master and spoke of William's feelings and instincts. There was no real evidence that the answer had anything to do with the pyramids or Egypt, but something was drawing the Lord High Bear to this as a possibility.

"Sorry Toomey, we can't be more specific than that, it's just a teddy bear feeling, in the pit of one's stomach that the answer is possibly here. You know that gut feeling that one can't shake off."

"I know it well and I would trust it without fail. Bear history chronicles uncountable occasions when intuition has been the crucial part of the solution or answer. Battles are won or lost on how keen is the gut feeling of Commanders. Do you have any clues that might be a starter for us to look at," asked Toomey.

"No, not really," replied Lexington. He changed position on the hard wooden chair and wriggled his ample rump to gain any extra comfort that he could find. "Except for what I have already told you and Beggrowgar's thought that it could be the place not a book that will help, we are stumped."

"Ok my friends, you have told me what you know and what you have seen. Now, tell me in your own words what your thoughts are about this light, even if it sounds silly or inconsequential. Anything, anything at all."

Coggrowgar hesitantly, thinking as he spoke started, "When I looked at the light a duo of morrows back, it seemed to me that it had brightened. It hadn't moved or grown, but the shimmering was brighter. It isn't hot, although no-one approaches too closely after what happened to Rugle and yet the trees are dying and the air around the castle is warming. Why?"

"You're right CG it is brighter and there is a very unkind feeling around it, it is constant, there all the time dayling and night-dark. Do you remember even Rugle said how uneasy he felt when he got close to it in flight?" agreed Lexington. "There is ill feeling felt by the Grand Master and all the senior bears. The adopted bears, so far, do not seem to be affected, but they are troubled and fearful by what they have seen and heard."

Lexington then smiled with pride and added, "But they are incredibly brave teddy bears, without their aid Rugle would have died of the cold once the heat had been sucked from him, they used their own bodies to keep in the warmth pumped in by four of the Trusted Bears. You paired for that didn't you CG?"

Coggrowgar nodded. "It was an honour to help our great friend."

Lexington now stood, unable to endure the too hard chair any longer. He padded to the far side of the room, relieving the tension in his rump as he did so.

"You have travelled over time and place CG do you have any further thoughts we can share?" Lexington was not sure what else to expect from this bear for whom he had immense respect. He had sailed under his command on a plentiful of journeys and was aware that Coggrowgar was more than capable of telling a tall tale, but he was also well versed in seabearship and was experienced in the ways of the worlds past and present, he also had strong views on the future.

Coggrowgar

Coggrowgar came to live at the castle following the battles with the Turks after being trapped on the Island of Malta. He remembered well the day he sailed into the bay at the head of his sailing ship, a proud captain and master of his vessel. He was greeted by Rugle with a roar that shook every plank on the ship. On that ship he carried the Grand Master and Lexington the Architect, as well as a small number of other bears.

He had enjoyed being the bear to one of the Knights Templar and as an experienced sailor had travelled from old England to the Crusades. He was also an accomplished horsebear having rode into battle with his knight. Bear Coggrowgar sustained a terrible wound across his leg in the battle with Saladin and was only treated by a ship's sail maker some morrows later. Today, he walks with a limp and when walking with Aiggrowgar they often compete to see who limps the best. Mostly, however, Coggrowgar walks tall and his manner is a style as though marching to the drum beat of war. When he is telling tales to the younger bears his heart aches a little with a yearning for the sea and battle action. He complains that it is disrespectful to be called Salty by the young bears, but as his fellow Trusted Bears know he enjoys the familiarity of being associated with his sailing times and loves to be asked to demonstrate the hornpipe.

Coggrowgar had been proud to be appointed one of the Trusted Bears and wore the responsibility with the ease of a bear familiar with the high office of captain. Honoured to be asked by the Grand Master to join Lexington the Master Architect on his journey to Egypt and excited at once again being able to sail, Coggrowgar now stood as an equal, looking at Lexington and Toomey who were awaiting his answer.

Slowly, as though he was about to tell a sea story to the adoption bears, Coggrowgar took a deep breath, stretched to the fullness of his imposing height and emptied his bear lungs in one go, his shoulders dropping as he did so.

"As you know Master Architect," he started in a respectful tone, "I've travelled the worlds, engaged in battles, feared for my life and seen bears lose theirs. I have experienced love and caring as well as hate and treachery. But I've long thought that there is a primary battle going on between the good elements and the not so good elements. I've never before needed to put it into words or explain it to anyone but, I feel that now we've been presented with the challenge of the light that this is possibly something to do with these two elements. Could it just be light vs. dark?"

"But dark is normally associated with the not so good side and light with the good," said Lexington.

"Yes, so I guess that would not make a lot of sense, but as Toomey just said, any thought no matter how daft it sounds."

"Quite right, I did CG and we all know things are not always what they seem, we've all been around in this teddy bear world of ours for long enough to have been puzzled quite a few times by what the universe has to show us. There must have been some reason that you have been drawn to this museum and what it can offer."

Toomey now paced the length of the room, turned, paced back and stopped where he had started. "I must look through some library books, ancient legends and some scientific data. You pair must be hungry, go eat in my quarters. There is a nicely simmering pot of grizzled sheep loins on the cooker. Eat your fill and come back here at middling time."

Feeling full and much more comfortable after the compulsory bout of burps, the trio regrouped in Toomey's office. Lexington rested against a bureau, avoiding the hard wooden chair.

“Now, how does the light come into all this? What is its role? I can find no previous reference to anything like this before. No legends, no recording of such an appearance, except.....”

The two bears angled their bodies towards Toomey, their interest and their fur aroused, “except, I found a very ancient, tattered scroll printed in Chinese hieroglyphics. There is a tale, just a tale though, about an old chinaman fleeing to Egypt and asking the Pharaoh for sanctuary. He was cared for and, as an elderly gentleman venerated, but whenever he was asked why he had left his home country, he would only ever answer ‘because of the bad light’. As far as I can ascertain, as said it is a very fragile, tattered document, no-one ever discovered to what he referred. There is no other mention of a light.” Toomey delicately, with frayed paws, placed the dark brown crumbling papyrus upon his desk. Lexington and Coggrowgar padded slowly towards it. The document was covered in the unfamiliar Chinese script, but it looked as one would imagine and old pirate map bearing clues to buried treasure – all crumbling edges and blackened holes.

Lexington looked across the desk at Coggrowgar, wonder and puzzlement shone fiercely from his eyes.

“I don’t understand,” he said, his muzzle twitching rapidly.

“Neither do I,” Toomey answered matter of factly in his brisk tone. “But that is all there is, maybe its importance, if there is any, will be revealed later when all the bears complete their searches. So I ask again what is the light for? Unless, as I now suspect……. unless... it is not light at all.”

“Not light!!” exclaimed Lexington and Coggrowgar in unison.

“Yes, that’s it,” said an animated Toomey, “not light as we know it. Light travels does it not? But you say this is a column over Wynghorran, it’s not travelling.” A triumphant Toomey beamed at the duo of startled bears. “It definitely is NOT light as we know it.”

“That would fit with what Winkington believes about the custard tart. But now, my old friend, we need to go,” said Lexington. “I can feel the Grand Master wants us back at the castle and, thanks to you both, we have some news to give him.”

Chapter 5 BEST LAID PLANS…..

When the Grand Master had asked the Major and Aiggrowgar to work together he had commented that although he was not sure of any specific help they could give at present, he was certain that the services and expertise of a duo of battle seasoned warriors would be needed. They were without question the best two to guard the castle and keep watch on any new developments. Winkington did not want any more surprises as had happened with the arrival of the light. The castle was on code indigo - high alert and Bearmont, as the major, had the responsibility of making sure that all the procedures and duties that accompanied code indigo were followed rigorously.

Bearmont was in his office checking the rotas when Aiggrowgar knocked on the massive oak door.

"Come!" shouted Bearmont without looking up.

The old warrior walked in and swung the door back on its heavy hinges. There was a hint of a squeak. "Needs oiling," muttered Aiggrowgar.

"So do I," was the wry reply. "Grab a chair and make yourself comfortable."

The battle-scarred bear chose the large well-worn armchair that he knew to be comfortable as he had sat in it many times before. He adjusted his eye patch and settled back, crossing his legs.

"Well my Old Pup," Aiggrowgar started, using the old familiar nickname by which he addressed the major, "another fine mess we find ourselves in." There was a pause.

"I think it's time for a goblet of mead, to get us thinking," said his host. The bears, close friends as well as rivals, mulled over what they knew about the problem mingled with tales and reminiscences of the past. There were many to choose from and the mead was helpful in fuelling the memory as well as the ability to exaggerate and exaggerate they did. Finally Bearmont remembering the reason for the meeting returned to discussing the light.

"Know what I think? I think we should find the switch and switch the thing off! Do you know where the switch is?" Another long pause, another sip of the mead.

"NOOOO," the slow growl came from Aiggrowgar.

"Then we'll just have to put it out, like a fire! Yep, that's it, just like a fire." Bearmont's eyes sparkled, he stood up, lumbered to the middle of the room and threw his arms wide, stretching his paws apart as wide as they would go. He started to whisper, conspiratorially.

"We get the castle fire engines, one each and we approach the light column from two opposite directions at high speed." He moved his arms inwards, gathering speed until his paws met with a huge thud. "And under the cover of darkness we blast the light with the high powered water cannons. The appliances have radios so we can coordinate the attack. We can use a secret code so I can send you a message and we can hit that light together."

He smacked his paws together again, with even more force this time. "We can annihilate that light, drive it back from whence it came. It will never withstand a double attack upon it. Why it isn't even solid, there is nothing to hold it here." In his excitement and eagerness Bearmont was now marching up and down the length of the small office, looking just like the caged bear that at that moment he was.

Aiggrowgar caught the major's passion and his fervour for the plan led him to visions of the glory that could be theirs. "You are right my Old Pup, the Grand Master and all the castle bears will be so proud of us. Imagine we might even get a Thank You Ceremony beside the Wisdom Tree."

At this thought both bears stopped moving, raised their heavy heads and looked at each other. A Wisdom Tree Ceremony was the highest accolade the Grand Master could bestow on a bear. A seriousness overtook them and they began to conceive a plan to put the mead inspired idea into action.

"Could we get the fire engines out of the fire station without too many questions being asked?"

"Yes," replied Bearmont, "we will tell the fire officer it is a secret mission that the Grand Master has entrusted to us. We will swear him to secrecy and ask him to instruct the firebears to set up the water cannons for us."

"Do we need to camouflage the engines in army greyling or something?"

"No we can come along the fore-shore over the sand, that will keep the noise down and obviously it will be a night-dark operation so no bear will see us. It'll just be the two of us, in fast, do the job and a quick exit before any bear realises what has happened.

“This is much better than just waiting about,” Aiggrowgar exclaimed. “This will be exiting, a real adventure again, at last. How soon should we carry it out?”

Bearmont looked at his time-piece, “It is eleventh of the night-grey, let us strike now. By the morrow the light pillar will be gone and the cubs can awake to proper sunshine once more.”

With a micro more of mead to warm them against the damp nightling airs the two bears left the office and hurried to the fire station at the bottom of the cliff.

The chief fire officer was sitting in the small watch-tower, drinking sweet tea. Long shifts during the night-dark had taught him that tea kept him awake and alert. Originally he had been an adoption bear but after scores of births he had sought permission from the Grand Master to remain at the castle. Leighton had fulfilled all his duties in his numerous lives with cheerfulness and compassion. Now he yearned for the company of his own kind and to have a home of his own. Winkington saw the weariness and yearning in the aged bear and granted him leave to stay. However, no bear can live at the castle for free and the Grand Master wished for Leighton to take on a role within the castle community.

“Tell me Leighton, what was your role in your last life among humans?” the Grand Master had enquired.

“I was the mascot of blue watch at the old Shoreditch fire station,” replied the worn bear. “I was born to my owner when he was but four boy years and all through the growing he wanted to be a fireman. By the time he was twenty-four he was the sub-officer at the station and I became the mascot for that watch. I rode to all the fires sitting on the dashboard looking out of the windscreen. It was a wonderful time.” The old bear smiled at these thoughts.

Winkington thoughtfully avoided asking Leighton how this life had come to a close, for he knew that leaving owners was sometimes extremely painful and he did not wish to inflict bad memories upon this bear, if any existed.

“Then we have a perfect solution,” beamed Winkington, “we need a new chief fire bear at the station, with your experience you are highly qualified. How about it, do you accept my offer?”

“Yes sir, I most certainly do.” Leighton stood to attention and saluted the Grand Master with the hairiest, longest bear arm that the Master had seen in many an era.

Thus it was Leighton who greeted those two incorrigible bears that night-dark when they arrived to ask for a brace of fire engines. The fire station had thrice fire engines lined up and shining like new pins. The engines were Dennis open cab-style with the large ladders suspended at an angle on the back of each appliance. They were impressive looking machines and the pride of Leighton's life. Bearmont explained that they needed two for the mission they had been ordered to carry out that very night. It was important that the ladders were removed and the water hose on each appliance fixed so that they could be operated without having to get out of the cab.

"It is imperative that the hoses are angled at 45 degrees on both engines," Bearmont went on, standing with his paws behind his back and feet astride, hoping that the military position he was adopting added to his authority. Although the Major always looked imposing he was acutely aware, unlike the fire chief, that a lot of creative licence was taking place here, even if it was for the good of the castle.

"I am a little concerned that you want the engines modified," stated Leighton, "after all you're not trained firebears and operating the engines is a skilled job. What if two of my bears drove for you?"

"I fully understand your hesitancy Fire Chief, after all they are magnificent machines and you keep them in immaculate condition," flattered Bearmont. "But as already explained this is a top secret mission and the least bears involved the better the chance of success. I know you understand Leighton. Orders must be obeyed."

Aiggrowgar had been standing a few paces back throughout this entire conversation, but he had been adding little 'mms', 'that's right's' and a few vigorous head nods hoping to add to the authenticity of the Major's story. He now asked his own question, giving the fire chief a friendly wink, which of course could not be interpreted as such because of his eye patch.

"We will need to borrow firebear helmets and jackets, it's cold out there this nightling. Can that be done? And, can you manage the modifications on your own or with just our help, as said we wish no-bear else to be involved?"

"No problem at all, gentleb'rs. I can certainly do as you ask singularly, it will take but a doubling of the hour, maybe less. You can get changed in our duty room and partake of some sweet tea to warm you for your task while you wait." Leighton stood and ushered the bears from the watch tower towards the duty room. He himself went immediately to the appliance bay to start the modifications, proud that he had been asked to play a small, but important part in the Grand Master's scheme that he imagined had something to do with the light.

"Ah, proper sweet tea," Bearmont said licking his lips and wiping his muzzle with the back of his paw.

"Not like the rubbish we were served in Palestine in the crusades, that was real rough tea. But then it was always hot." Aiggrowgar replied helping himself to another mugful. "Ok what exactly is this ambitious plan of yours?"

“We will place ourselves a duo of furlongs away from the column in opposite directions, without lights and then we will drive towards the column at a quince of paces per micro until we are just a middle furling from the column edge. Then, in tandem, we both start up our water cannons and put out that light. Let’s synchronise our timepieces now.” Both checked their pocket chronometers.

“Ready?”

“Ready, let’s go.” Off marched the two happy teddy bears with not a sign of fear for the dangers that may lie ahead. Two fearless warriors, ready in mind and body, the do or die saviours of the castle, heroes of the morrow.

“This will go down in history,” said Bearmont.

“Written up in books I expect,” added Aiggrowgar as they made their way to the appliance bay to collect the bright scarlet, trusty steeds they would soon be riding into battle.

The fire chief explained that he had set the hoses at the right angle and that once they hit the pump start button the water would keep going until the large water tanks emptied. This would allow them to concentrate on anything else they had to do. Climbing aboard Bearmont thanked Leighton for his help and the two bears drove silently across the sands guided only by the light from the far away column. They waited, engines running, time-pieces at the ready for the paws to reach the middle dozen.

GO….. the bears double declutched the gears and raced the engines towards the target at the agreed speed. When a middle furling from the column edge they skidded to a halt and at the very same micro reached forward and hit the water pump start buttons. What happened next will never be included in any tales that these two storytelling warriors would relate in the future. As the water jet shot from each hose and hit the light, the column opened as quickly as a double door to a honey shop. The water went straight through the light column and across to the cab of the opposite fire engine. The two astonished and fast becoming very wet bears were now sitting up to their waists in water as the cabs filled and then over flowed, water cascading from the machines turning them into grotesque imitations of the grandest fountains that stood in Rome.

Wet, bedraggled, cold and feeling humbled the two bears who returned the fire engines to the station, showed a very different appearance to the astonished Leighton who was again sworn to secrecy and ordered never to discuss the episode ever again. Not even between themselves and certainly not to the Grand Master. In silence Aiggrowgar and Bearmont, lumbered along the track towards the castle leaving a water trail in their heavy pawsteps. A double dose of hot ginger wine laced with honey would be the only thing to warm their sodden bodies and their dispirited hearts.

Unbeknown to the bears one spectator had watched every move and heard every word that had occurred that night-dark. Rugle, still recuperating, had been sleeping around his beloved rock when the bears had first walked along the fore-shore. Without moving, for he still bore aching bones and limbs, he had opened his eyes and watched the unfolding pantomime. The dragon swore for ever after that laughter was indeed the best medicine and was convinced his convalescence had been shortened because of it by at least a trio of morrows. He was just a little bit sad in his mirth that he would never be able to thank his fine friends for helping to make him well again.

Plan B

A morrowmarch later Aiggrowgar sat once more in Major Montgomery's office, once again he was stretched out in the old armchair. Initially the two warriors had been glum but realised they had been lucky to have kept the details of the fire engine escapade from the Grand Master. Now, as always, Bearmont had returned to his jolly self and had begun plans for another attempt at ridding Bear World and the castle of the light. After all he was the military guardian of the castle and had promised to spend all his time endeavouring to keep every bear and everything safe. This time he had approached Winkington about his plan and discussed his idea to blow up the pillar of light. The Grand Master had queried whether it was possible to blow something up that was not made of solid material. The Major had shaken his head and explained that he really did not know but he felt they had to do something. Being pro-active would at least keep everyone occupied so the bears would feel as if things were happening and, most importantly, it would stop them from being worried and eventually afraid. Winkington agreed with this philosophy and asked Bearmont to use whatever resources he felt necessary.

"Well," said Bearmont, explaining to his occupied friend, "I've decided we are going to blow this thing up, we have the dynamite at the back of Rugle's cave. It's been there a long time, it was used when the castle foundations were laid. But Rugle and I have inspected it and it's still in good, useable condition."

"OK, sounds a good plan my Old Pup," mumbled Aiggrowgar slurping his way through a bagful of dates. He was keeping an eye on his weight and desperately trying to cut down on the number of honeycombs he could eat in a seventh period. Vanity was not part of Aiggrowgar's mindset, but extra weight to carry on his scarred and shortened leg caused him difficulties. "But how do we get the dynamite into the column? Won't we have to get it right in the middle and high up? Could we use a ladder?"

"Don't be daft," laughed Bearmont, "what would we lean it against! I was thinking more of a rocket like the Chinese used in the 3rd dynasty. Bear William will have details of something that could help us somewhere in that library of his."

"Sounds a bit risky and we don't have a lot of time. The light is brightening every dayling now, even the adoption bears are starting to notice."

"Well what about a glider then, the plans of a flying machine that daVinci drew are also in the library," said Bearmont.

"What fly over and drop the dynamite in!" Aiggrowgar shook his head. "No that wouldn't work, remember Rugle couldn't find the top and it wouldn't be safe to get too near the light after what happened to him." Aiggrowgar shook his paper bag to see if any dates had got stuck in the corners, he was suddenly aware that he had probably eaten the last one. He peered with his good eye, holding the bag up to his face. No luck, it was empty.

"Yes, my friend, you are right, so how then?" Bearmont cradled his head in his white paws this was his 'help I don't know the answer' position.

Aiggrowgar now giving his full attention back to the

quandary that confronted them asked, "What if we load up the glider with the dynamite and fly it into the column about half a league up? But what do we use for an engine? Nope, can't think of anything."

Bearmont looked up with renewed interest, "But gliders don't have engines! We must find another way to get it airborne.....a big catapult? Hmm, that could be risky."

"Not if we put a pilot in the glider and he parachuted out just before the glider went into the column. OOOH shivering mackerel but that sounds dangerous for the pilot. Who would want to do it?"

"But it's the best idea we've come up with so far. OK, this is what we do." Bearmont continued, "Let's put the word out to all bears that we are looking for a very brave bear to undergo a secret mission that is of the utmost secrecy and will be dangerous." The incongruity of his sentence escaped him in his enthusiasm. "Great, once more we have a plan AG. This has been a good dayling's work.

Word went around the castle on the whisper-whisper network. It was in a blink of a butterfly that there was a knock on Bearmont's great door.

"Come," shouted Bearmont and through the door walked a very scruffy looking bear.

"You want a bear for a secret, dangerous mission?" a squeaky voiced asked.

"That we do, that we do," replied Bearmont recognising the scruffy creature before him as a recent arrival on the west wing. "And what's your name?"

"Denny the Dustcart Bear is my full name. That's because I was one of those bears that finish up riding on the front bumper of a dustcart. Working for Dover County Council I was, me and my owner Lightening Louis, legendary he was, could empty bins quicker than anyone else in the depot. Why one day.........."

Bearmont interrupted quickly, fearing this could turn into a very long interview if he didn't take control.

"Yes ok Denny, now just tell me why you think you are suited for our dangerous mission?"

"I fell off the bumper and went under that dust cart more times that I care to remember," explained Denny demonstrating a beautiful agile backwards roll to show how he had escaped from the giant wheels of the cart. "So is this mission any more dangerous than that?"

Bearmont chortled at the little scruffy bear and took an immediate fancy to the plucky cub. "No, I don't think it is more dangerous than that. You'll do a treat as our pilot Denny, but please remember it's top secret, so keep this appointment to yourself and come back after middle dayling and we will fill you in with all the details."

"Well done Denny for volunteering," Aiggrowgar added slapping the little cub on the back sending him hurtling through the door. "See you later."

As Denny left, scuttling down the long corridor and twisted staircases, back to the west wing to tell the other adoption bears he had been chosen to take part in a top secret, dangerous mission, Bearmont and Aiggrowgar turned to each other and growled hearty belly laughs until they were hoarse.

"Whatever next AG," Bearmont gasped, "but, I do believe we are now ready for our next attack."

The old friends switched their minds into battle mode and left the office. Bearmont went to seek out William in the library and ask if there was a drawing of the daVinci flying machine. Aiggrowgar climbed down to Rugle's cave to locate the dynamite. They were to meet as soon as possible at the wood workshop behind the conservatory at the end of the Great Hall. When Aiggrowgar arrived the Major was already in deep conversation with Woodrow the chief carpenter, no longer just a nickname because of his trade, his real name had long been forgotten over the ages of time. Aiggrowgar moved over to the work-bench and studied the drawings of the flying machine that Bearmont had obtained, taking note of the conversation about the preparation needed to get a glider up and running. Bearmont was promising Woodrow as many paws as he needed to get the project completed and in position on the fore-shore on the north side of the castle. The carpenter promised to also get the lower workshop organized for the making of the giant catapult.

Back at Bearmont's office the scruffy little cub was waiting for them. The two senior bears explained to Denny how they planned to get a flying machine made and catapult it towards the light column. The flight would start some distance back from the light so the correct launch angle would be achieved. The plane would be loaded with the dynamite but it needed a pilot who could guide the plane to the right height and light the fuse before parachuting to safety.

"Any questions?" Bearmont asked the little bear who had listened silently throughout the briefing.

"When do my flying lessons start" said Denny with a big grin on his face.

The Assault

The catapult was the first part of the attack equipment to be ready and was dragged out onto the fore-shore, a league from Rugle's cave but still well back from the light column. Aiggrowgar was organising the many bears who had come out to help.

"We need to secure the catapult firmly to the ground, pin it down with bolts so there is no movement when launching. It needs to line up directly facing the column and then we will be ready to load the flying machine."

Many eras before Aiggrowgar had worked with soldiers building medieval siege weapons. He had been fascinated by the trebuchet, similar to a catapult and designed to throw large heavy objects at castles to destroy them. He thus knew it was vital to line up the projection angle exactly or the glider would miss the column altogether and the mission would fail.

Bearmont was still with Woodrow in the workshop, working hurriedly but methodically, overseeing the adoption bears who had each been paired with a wood-shop bear in order to get the part of the flying machine allocated to them, completed and ready for the big assembly. The excitement in the workshop was tangible and the teddy bears had gladly undertaken the difficult work pleased to be helping with the secret mission known throughout the castle. Aiggrowgar made his way up from the fore-shore to the workshop to see if he could help in any way. The catapult had been positioned and secured to his satisfaction and he was eager to now secure the glider in place. Purposeful in his strides the old warrior was at his most efficient when planning and executing a campaign. Routine or lazy days were an irritant to him, for they were the times that his old wounds troubled him most. Any bear observing him now on his climb to the workshop, with the characteristic tilt of his head, would not have seen a limp at all.

On the narrow path he met Bearmont on his way down to the fitters shop to see if Denny's parachute was ready and packed. The little cub had already had a fitting for the harness and been shown how to operate the straps to eject himself from the glider. Everything was complete and Bearmont said Denny would be along within a fourth of the hour to collect everything.

By middle dayling the bears had gathered at the shore with their glider components ready to be assembled and set into the catapult. There could be no test run, everyone present was keenly aware that getting it right first time was the only option. Denny was pacing up and down not sure if it was nerves or just eagerness to get on with the mission that was making his brave heart beat a doubling of its usual timing. Rugle, watching all the preparations from his customary laying place, had spoken to the plucky bear about the delights of flight.

"First, you will soar upwards into the sky, this is when you will feel the primary g-force. Do not be alarmed, it will pass in a micro. Then you will have just a short period in which to fly silently above us all towards the target. You will be anxious as it is your only time, but enjoy the exhilaration, the silence of flight, the wind swooping over your fur, the view......everything about the adventure. Nothing you have ever done or will do in future time will ever compare with it. You alone will be privileged to experience and feel as I feel when I fly. You are a brave bear, my little friend, my hearts will be with you and I will await your return."

This was the first time Denny had ever spoken to the dragon and the encounter raised his excitement to even greater heights. Rugle had assured him that he would return safely. His ego was also boosted for very few of the ordinary teddy bears got to have an audience with the dreaded dragon. Rugle would have welcomed them, but his presence and size inspired awe rather than friendliness and somehow it had become custom that only the senior bears befriended the only remaining dragon.

The Trusted Bears, except for Duggrowsar, had brought the dynamite up from the cave, stacked it and loaded it into the flying machine that had now been assembled. The Grand Master had ordered that it was too dangerous for the adoption and workshop bears to risk their health carrying the explosive. All went well and the octet micro fuse was set and made ready for Denny to pull immediately before he ejected a score of bear paces from the column. If the calculations were correct the dynamite filled glider would explode in the centre of the column, half a league up and out would go the light, blasted to smithereens.

With the entire company of bears watching the Major and Aiggrowgar carefully, with tender paws, helped the pilot into the glider making sure he was comfortable. There was no need to strap in him for he would only be in the cockpit for a score of micros. Bearmont went over the drill with Denny for the final time and then patting him on the head, Bearmont shuffled back and withdrew from the glider.

Denny was now alone, being dragged ever backwards as the catapult was wound up. The adrenalin rush made his head feel a little woozy and his muzzle dry. He clasped his gloved paws together for he wished no observer, especially Duggrowsar, to see the slight tremor that was occurring. He thought of Rugle's words and was comforted. This after all was an adventure, for all of its seriousness, to be enjoyed. With all the bears winding the mechanism to pull the catapult as taut as possible, the air was heavy with grunts and deep throated gasps. Bearmont had his hand on the catapult trigger, it was now or never.

'CLICK'. Swooooosssshh, the flying machine was away, whistling through the air. Every bear on the fore-shore inhaled a deep breath and looked upwards, their dark eyes following the rising projectile. The glider shot up at the correct angle accompanied by silence and a holding of breath. The many eyes were focussed on the single object, suddenly there were two and all realised that Denny had left the flying machine, his chute opened and...... splooosh! Not a bang, or a shot, or a crack...... just a splooooosh accompanied by thousands of timber splinters raining down on the castle, the fore-shore and the astonished bears, who now quickly covered their eyes from the fast falling debris.

In a never could be imagined result, the column had just absorbed the explosion, sort of eaten it was the only way they could later describe it. All the bears stood open muzzled, confused, unable to comprehend the event they had just witnessed. Bearmont and Aiggrowgar just looked at each other; no words were spoken or needed. The disappointment was evident in their body language and shaking heads.

Denny, who had landed safely, was slowly making his way back, half-carrying half-dragging his parachute, to the gathering that surrounded the now empty catapult.

.

.

Chapter 6 DECISIONS

The Grand Master had called the senior and the Trusted Bears to the Spell-room. As always the room was quiet but sadly no longer smelt of honey popcorn and warm air. The bears stood pensively around the table waiting for Winkington. It would have been normal for the bears when coming together to chat and exchange salutations, but on this occasion no-one spoke. They had arrived, taken their places around the table and awaited the arrival of the Grand Master. They did not have to wait long.

"Firstly, I would like to inform you that Rugle is well on the way to recovery, thanks to the efforts of you all and especially to Dooey. Thank you. Welcome back bears that have been away." Winkington then positioned himself into the upright Queen Anne style chair and the other bears followed gratefully.

He then continued, "Since we last met I have spent time in meditation with the Wisdom Tree. I have reached the conclusion that I must listen to you all very carefully as the answer to our challenge is within the castle, of that I am certain."

Winkington looked around at these bears for whom he had a never-ending love and respect. He was firmly of the opinion that the answer lay with one or more of these true friends who had, of their own free will, lived together for an age that had no beginning that anyone of them could remember.

"I will go around the table and ask each of you if you have managed to discover anything or have any thoughts on our situation. I hope that by asking you one at a time we will not miss any little clue or snippet of information that you have discovered. If we all listen to each other then we may find that we are already aware of an important factor but the bear who knows it may not recognise it as such," Winkington smiled at his close allies, "have I made myself clear?"

The eight bears nodded and grunted their acknowledgement.

"Bearmont," began the Grand Master, "I know that you and Aiggrowgar have made a duo of attempts to destroy the column."

On hearing their names, both bears looked up startled at the mention of both attacks on the light.

“Not much happens here at Wynghorran without me knowing comrades,” smiled Winkington, wrinkling his nose, “but then me thinks you already know that.”

He directed his gaze upon Bearmont again and continued, “I know you have walked the castle inside and out with Lexington; sorry Lex, a lot to ask on top of your Egyptian trip, but time is of the essence. As the architect and builder of the castle you have the eyes to help Bearmont notice any changes or any weaknesses occurring.”

And so it was for the third time that Winkington looked again at Montgomery, “Tell me Bearmont, were you able to discover anything that could assist us in our challenge?”

“Grand Master we have walked the castle inside; its rooms, halls and corridors. Outside we checked the walls and gates as well as the gardens and down to the fore-shore. We opened our hearts as well as our minds in the hope that something would show itself to us. The only obvious damage is one of the toffee scented window panes in the west wing has a small crack in it. I’m unsure if that is an effect of the light or merely a coincidence. The crack is however new. In the gardens and orchards the trees are now completely bare and the grass, as you know, has crisped and browned. The bees also appear very sluggish and the honey count is down quite considerably. Apart from that I don’t have anything to report from the search." Bearmont, who had stood straight-backed while talking, now gave a short nod and sat down.

Lexington quickly interspersed, "Sorry to disagree Bearmont, but I do think you have something else to add. As Winkington said, maybe we will not always see the importance of something ourselves, but do you remember when we were in the rest room in the centre tower? You said you detected a different feeling to that in the rest of the castle and grounds."

"Yes, you're right I did, but it was just a passing comment, I didn't think anything of it." Bearmont answered.

"Neither did I at the time, as I felt nothing, but having given some thought to everything we saw I realised that I too used to feel like that." Lexington sighed, "It was so long ago when we built the castle my thought had faded, but when we built the tower it did feel different. I put it down to the fact that it was the first tower to be constructed and that made it special, almost like it was the heart of the castle. But, I digress, Bearmont could you try to explain the feeling you had in more detail? It could be important."

All the bears leant slightly forward, intrigued to hear what Bearmont had to say as everyone was more than aware that the castle spoke to Bearmont on his nightling patrols. This could prove to be a vital clue.

Winkington extended an open paw towards the major indicating that he too wished the bear to continue.

"Thanks Lex I will try. When we entered the centre tower it felt safe…… and different, in a good way. It didn't seem unusual at the time, but you are right it was noticeable enough for me to have mentioned it to you. I can best describe it as in some way it was protective of me, protecting me from the bad. If that makes sense Grand Master"

"Not yet it doesn't my friend," laughed Winkington, "but your feelings about the castle are always important and we will collate this information with all the other facts we can discover. Somewhere it will all fit together, like the ingredients for a cake, once we see them mixed together we will know what cake it is and then we will understand. OK let's move on."

The Grand Master sipped the apple cordial in front of him, cleared his throat and turned his gaze towards Coggrowgar. "How did you and Lexington get on in Egypt?"

"I have a feeling," Coggrowgar began, "that this thing that Bearmont spoke of about right and wrong has some bearing on my thoughts. When Lex and I had a conversation with Toomey in Cairo this feeling of good and not so good came up then. I've for much time felt that the good and bad are now fighting each other in open conflict. But I questioned my own thoughts as they were vague. Maybe being in the environment of the great museum with all the history and magnitude that goes with the museum on display, one's mind opens up more clearly to many possibilities. Trying to explain my thoughts to others did make them more concise."

Lexington added Toomey's explanation that the light was not just light; it contained unidentified elements, just as Winkington had first thought. If they could identify them they could fight them. All the bears sat silently, knowing that indeed this was the task before them. Trying to fight the light without understanding of how it was composed was futile, as Bearmont and Aiggrowgar had discovered. Sipping the apple cordial and helping themselves to the copious amounts of peppered pork popcorn displayed in large crystal bowls spread around the table, gave them all time to reflect without a noticeable pause in the conversation.

Scribbling on her pad, noting relevant details for herself, Duggrowsar's head shot up when Lexington recounted Toomey's story about the Chinese mandarin. With the thick felt pen she marked a large exclamation mark upon her pad, covering the length of the page and on either side she wrote the word 'legend'. The female bear then turned her attention back to the assembled bears and patiently waited for her own turn to speak.

Aiggrowgar looking pensive adopted his story telling posture. "Grand Master you asked me to work alongside Bearmont and to help him in his duty to protect yourself, the bears and the castle. As you are aware," he gave a wry smile and continued, "we made a couple of attempts to fight the column but to no avail. Since we last met I have visited every corner of the castle, every battlement and all the grounds surrounding the castle and I find nothing that concerns me as a point of weakness. I've looked and studied the column of light so many times. I've walked to the fore-shore so that I was able to see it from outside and I used a magnifying glass to intensify the light onto a piece of paper to see what sort of heat would be generated. There was nothing. I find this extremely puzzling. I have not had a chance to discuss this with Bearmont or Eaggrowgar our scientist, but I told myself, this column, it is not just light otherwise it would be hot and it would heat. I suppose I'm really just saying I agree with the rest of you."

"That's very interesting, AG. Yes, if it was just light it would have heated the paper through the magnifying glass. You have confirmed our thoughts. Well done," smiled Eaggrowgar slapping his friend on the back. "Well done."

"Thank you AG most useful, most useful indeed. Now William and BG what can you add?" asked Winkington.

"We have been very busy liaising with Lexington since his return from Egypt, as well as with the continuing rise in the number of spell requests that we are getting from our bears from all parts of man-world. We've noticed the type of spell requests are mostly to deal with the effects on the family life of humans. It appears to be a rapidly changing world out there Grand Master."

"This sounds disturbing William, very disturbing," said Winkington his concern sounding in his voice. "I feel that we need to look at this closer. I would ask you to give some thought to it and maybe ask some of the newly arrived adoption bears for their thoughts and get back to me. I knew that there was a change, that I had picked up on the camera obscura, but I was not aware that it had got so bad."

Winkington gave a large deep throated belch, wiped his muzzle with his long black tongue and focused his attention on the only lady bear seated amongst them.

"Dooey I thank you exceedingly for the help you gave to our great friend Rugle. That he was so injured abiding to my request troubled me. Thanks to you and your knowledge he is well on course to recovery."

Duggrowsar spoke softly but clearly, her eyelashes blinking rapidly as she fought the embarrassment of being singled out for thanks. She knew she had only played a part and every bear at the castle had aided the dragon's swift healing. "I thank you Grand Master for your thoughts. I have spoken to Rugle and he will return to complete fitness within a few more morrows. He's only too sorry that his venture gained no advantage for us, but he was and is eager to help in our quest to banish the light column."

"Good, good. Now to return to our mission, have you anything to add to these thoughts of ours re the light?"

"I have indeed. As you are all aware I spent much of my early life in China and having spoken in depth with Rugle and listened to you all today, especially you Lex, I wish to tell you a story that I heard from an old martial arts master during the 3rd dynasty in China. Back then stories were the only way of passing on knowledge to the populace and I loved the Chinese wisdom and morality of their stories. I have come to appreciate that they're just as relevant in today's world and this one may help us."

The eight bears, despite the variegations in their sizes and shapes all shifted as one. Settling in and getting comfortable for a good story was an innate teddy bear quality. However serious the occasion a story telling was to be enjoyed.

Duggrowsar, after a quantious slug of cordial began. "The wise martial arts master told his young students about 'The Great Battle of life and death that goes on inside all human beings'. The wise man said the battle is between two Dragons….they eternally battle for dominance inside us all. One is dark, it represents Evil. It is anger, envy, jealousy, sorrow, vengeance, greed, arrogance, self pity and ego.

The other is light. It represents Good. It is joy, love, peace, hope, kindness, truth, generosity, and compassion. The students who were listening attentively, waited for the story to continue, but the wise man just sat watching them. They thought for a while and then one of the students asked, 'But Master which Dragon wins?' The wise old man simply replied - The One You Feed."

William entranced by the transparency of the story said, "How simple, how true. Do you think that is what's happening here?"

Duggrowsar nodded thrice, "We know that although the light forms a large column over part of the castle and the grounds it has not attacked or harmed any of us," she paused then continued, "and yet it did attack Rugle. My friends I have come to the conclusion that the light in some way 'saw' Rugle as the good dragon and so attacked him. I believe the light to be a representation of the bad dragon."

Loud gasps came from every quarter of the table. Like the Chinese master's story, Duggrowsar's theory was simple, precise and made sense. "Bears, listening to you today has helped me turn my muddled, many thoughts into clear thoughts, but I do not know how we challenge the light."

"If we know what we are fighting, then we will find a way to defeat the light. We have made great progress here today my friends. I am well pleased with our endeavours. We all, I am sure, recognise the truth in Dooey's idea. Now we must devise our plan. What has brought about this manifestation is still not clear and we will investigate further, but |I am now sure that the light contains man's ills. Onwards comrades we have much to do." The Grand Master smiled at each bear individually, then, as they rose from their chairs Winkington embraced each one in a bone crunching bear hug and marched off, leaving the squashed bears to re-shake back out their crumpled fur.

The Grand Master

Winkington's bone crunching muscles had been honed by the fires of the blacksmith's brazier. Apprenticed as a young cub his life was centred within the open-sided forge that occupied the core of the village. His heartbeat throbbed with the rhythm of the huge hammer he wielded above his head and swung in an arc, sparking and thundering upon the hot iron as he shaped it. Time upon time the hammer fell accurately, steadily and with even weight. In the early years the acrid smoke stung his eyes as the sizzling foamy water sprayed his fur and the object emerged from its fiery birth. Amid the din, heat and metallic smells daily, yearly, Winkington worked learning his craft, learning about bears and learning that this was what he wanted to do for the rest of his life. He was content, complete and utterly wrong as to where his future lay.

Everybear in the village and surrounding hamlets used the Smithy regularly. Bear World passed through the forge and with each customer Winkington learnt. Many warriors came: for armour, for horseshoes, for swords but fewer returned after the battles. The young bear reasoned battles were a last resort, futile in their glory.

Farmers brought their ploughs to be mended and Winkington crafted their wheel bonds and naves and fitted them to the cartwheels. He saw how shared hard work with neighbours made life more comfortable for all involved.

Girl bears wearing flower necklaces, came in small giggling groups with their broken handled pots and bread to be baked in the stone box next to the forge. He recognized how their friendship strengthened them. The young cubs watched him and the braver ones asked questions: what was this tool called? What was this one used for? How did he keep the fire going? Winkington rejoiced in the young ones thirst for knowledge and eagerness to please.

As the young apprentice grew to bearhood his skills sharpened along with his teeth and keen eyesight. His back broadened and his shoulders bore the weight of the burdens gradually being placed upon them. Winkington's skill spread beyond his own boundaries. His mastery of alloying the iron with carbon made his crucible steel the most sought after, for with it he produced the keenest cutting edge in all the North Land.

His knowledge grew beyond his blacksmith's skills as he was needed to be dentist, doctor, undertaker and vet. As blacksmith he was the very heart of the village and as such was learned in numeracy, metallurgy and business skills. Winkington held one of the most important offices in the district that of Magistrate and his justice was tempered with fairness, respect and fellowfeel.

Life was good and the daylings blended one upon another. The morrows held surprises but never life-changing incidents until the dayling the stranger entered his ordered world.

Singing loudly to himself as he worked, the sweating bear was engrossed in pumping the bellows to obtain the maximum heat from the charcoal fire within which he was melting small pieces of iron ore to make his first 'bloom' of the day. Winkington was pondering on whether to turn this into a duo of arrow heads or if there would be enough to make the scraper the stone-mason had requested when there came a loud shout from outside. Two voices could then be heard loud and excited, or perhaps even frantic Winkington mused as he laid the bellows aside, straightened his back and wiped his darkened paws on the cloth tied around his middle. His glance into the bright outside saw a dark shape galloping on all fours towards him. The bear who had obviously just directed him was now watching the large shaggy bear until he reached the Smithy.

"Come quick please, he said you could help." The shaggy bear now stood upright and was pointing at the still staring bear. "I fear my master is gravely injured, he is trapped under the cart. Please, please come."

Winkington, having idly picked up his hammer now dropped it onto the anvil and followed the bear across the square, out of the village and back up the track. He asked no name for this was an urgent cry for help; a bear was hurt and needed aid. The duo now racing side by side skirted the woods and rounded the bend. Digging his heels into the soft earth to accomplish a rapid stop Winkington could see the overturned carriage and a bear crouched over the broken wagon that had tumbled half into the ditch. As he closed the distance between them he could hear the bear was talking to someone beneath the wagon. Both bears, out of breath from galloping, could not momentarily speak but approached the broken carriage. Winkington could see the lower part of a well-built bear protruding out from under the twisted wreckage. Kneeling down on all fours he leaned closely in and spoke to the hidden bear.

"Can you hear me?"

"Yes I can hear you," came the quiet reply.

"Can you tell me, is anything broken?"

"I don't believe so but the carriage is on top of me and I can't move."

Winkington hastily checked over the wagon, his keen eyes searching for any imminent danger. He bent down and looked as far under the carriage as he could. For just a few micros he thought and then gave his instructions to the two companions standing by. Even in the emergency he noted the anxiety on the bears' faces and spoke calmly and very clearly.

"I am going to lift the cart. When I shout 'now' I want you to grab a paw each and pull your friend well clear of the carriage. Do make sure that he is well clear because when I let go it will come down with a crash". The duo nodded and moved to the required position. The bear trapped beneath had also heard the instructions and straightened his paws ready to be grabbed.

Winkington placed his broad back as close to the wagon as he could, spread his hind paws solidly into the soft ground and settled in. Grabbing firmly the side of the wagon Winkington addressed the two companions.

"Are you ready?"

"Yes we're ready."

He could see they had bent as close as they could to their friend ready to grab and pull.

Winkington took the strain, "One...two...three... LIIIIFT."

And lift he did, with all his strength flowing through him he held on as the weight of the cart moved off the trapped bear.

"NOW," shouted Winkington. With a quick scurry the bear was pulled free.

"We've got him, we've got him, he's free." The shout was heard in unison. Winkington let go but as he did a splinter jutting out from the side of the damaged cart caught his arm and a vivid gash appeared that began to bleed profusely.

Winkington wrapped a soiled rag around his forearm, gasped for breath and informed the travelling companions that he would take the hurt bear back to the village. Scooping the wounded bear up in his arms Winkington and the thankful bear winced together. Through pain the smile became a grimace. Balancing his awkward burden the Blacksmith spoke to the bear he could now see for the first time.

"Hold tight my friend, it's but a short distance to the village."

At a slow but steady pace the carried and the carrier made their way back to the village, the duo of agitated bears following a few paces behind.

"What is your name my friend?"

"Gerald."

"Your shoulder is bleeding heavily Gerald, it hurts?"

"A little, but you're bleeding as well. I'm not sure whose blood is whose." The grimace smiles this time were more strained.

As they entered the village a small group of bears gathered to see if they could help in any way. Winkington carried the now shivering bear to the forge and rested him on a bench close to the warm fire. Gently prodding at the sodden shoulder fur Winkington examined the deep puncture wound.

"I need to cauterise your wound with this iron Gerald." Winkington shoved the black metal into the heart of the forge and the flames sparkled. "It will hurt for a few moments but it will clean and stop the bleeding. I'm sorry my friend."

The bear on the bench gritted his teeth exposing the jagged edges and nodded. As Winkington picked up the flaming iron, like one of his own hammer blows the knowledge hit him as an explosion in his head...the concern...the deference shown by this bear's companions...the name....this was none other than the Grand Master himself. Winkington turned and plunged the iron deep into the shoulder and branded Gerald: Grand Master of Bear World.

The recovering bear was ready to leave, his carriage repaired by Winkington. He watched as one of his companions, adjusted the harness and checked the shafts.

"I have enjoyed immensely our few daylings Winkington, it has given me the opportunity to observe village life once again and to spend time with the bears here. You are thought of highly young bear for your achievements."

"Thank you Sire, I too have enjoyed your forced stay, but I regret it was an accident that made it possible."

Gerald guffawed, a full throaty resonance echoing around the smithy. "The carriage tumbling in this place on that dayling was no accident my friend. It is the sign for which I have long sought. Our blood has mingled young cub and you will now be known as my designate."

"But I am just a village blacksmith Grand Master, I know nothing of learning," replied a very startled Winkington who had come to a very abrupt stop on their walk to the carriage.

"Tshh," said Gerald with a backwards wave of his good arm. "Books can be read, but life must be lived, must be experienced. This you have done."

"Grand Master this is a great honour you offer me, but I am not ready. I do not know if this is something I can do."

Gerald smiled and placed his paw on Winkington's arm. "Ahh, but it is my job to know if this is something you can do. And I say yes."

He paused and with rheumy eyes looked straight at Winkington. "As for being ready that is easy, when you can tell me why Good and Bad are the same then you must come and find me, for then you will be ready and I will be tired. Work hard my Apprentice, we will meet again."

Gerald clambered into the carriage and his companions drove him away as an astonished Winkington stood in the market place and watched the wagon diminish from sight.

A thousand daylings later the Blacksmith left the village to walk to the East Land in search of the Grand Master's dwelling. He now knew that as with Hero and Villain; Hate and Love, Good and Bad were never that simple. They were complex, multi-layered and held together by the middle rein. They were not opposites they were just extremes of the same and emotions would travel from one end to another, hovering somewhere along the continuum until, fed by circumstance, they moved to one side or the other.

Adoption Bears pretending to be William & Aiggrowgar

Chapter 7 THE ADOPTION BEARS

"O.K. Beggrowgar, tell me what you have discovered from our records. Have things changed noticeably for the adoption bears?" asked William.

They were seated in his small study, just off the Spell-room. It was probably the most conventionally built room in the castle. Oak panels covered the walls, the Jacobean ceiling was magnificent in its intricate designs and borders and the flooring was solid Canadian pine. It was, however, the windows that distinguished the room and made it unique. William had chosen beveled windows that looked like they had been stolen from a Victorian sweet shop. Lattice with bottle ended glass panes, although, of course, built long before the Victorians ever existed. William had spent time in Venice with the original glass making families who had guarded their secret of glass and mirror making, even from their fellow Venetians, for centuries. He had been fascinated by the skill and technique used by these master craftsmen, who had learnt the craft of glass making from emigrating Arabian families generations before. Glass, in all its varied shapes, colours and forms had occupied William's free periods for many eras. It was he who had installed the camera obscura in the library and in the private domain of his study stood a very large telescope, that had informed, delighted and amused William over many a nightling when sleep would not come.

"Two things appear to be going on," replied Beggrowgar. "The requests for spells have increased doublefold over the past duo of years. I knew it had increased but I didn't realize by how much. The other significant find I've made is that these requests are coming from a smallish group of adoption bears. A large proportion of bears out there in man-world we are not hearing from at all.

"That's strange," said William, "I certainly hadn't noticed that the requests were not evenly spread. Very remiss of me. Has this also been over the past duo?"

"No, it pre-dates that. Like you I knew our work-load had risen, but I had not picked up on the fact that the requests were only from a certain section of bears. I've looked at the records and amazingly we are not hearing from well over half of the bears out there."

"What - half!! That's impossible, surely," exploded William. "Are you sure?"

"Yes, William, I'm sure. I've checked, rechecked and checked again. I could not believe it myself. Neither could I believe that we hadn't noticed before now. I'm really sorry."

"Sorry, no. It's my fault; I should have picked this up before. Have you any explanation for this BG?"

"I can only presume that because of the increased work-load, we just didn't take much notice from whom the requests were coming."

"Mmmm, I suppose we are only hubears and not infallible. Still, I'm not sure what the Grand Master will think of our efficiency when we explain it to him! And, we still don't have an explanation for why over half of the adoption bears are not contacting us at all. Surely, it can't mean they are not fulfilling their duties. No! I can't believe that. But….what reason can there be?"

"William," Beggrowgar said gravely, "I can only think of one reason. Like you, I do not believe our bears would not fulfill their duties. No, the only reason I can think of….and I don't know how to say this, but..... the only reason I can think of is that...um...our bears are not being born."

"By the Great Grizzly, surely not. Adoption bears out there not being born!! I don't know what to say," William stood up. He walked to the window and looked out. The bottle shaped glass distorted the view, but his vision was not focused on the ground outside. He was deep in thought. His vision was misted and vague, a world where half the adoption bears were not born was too terrifying to imagine.

"Beggrowgar my friend, we must investigate this immediately. Something is seriously wrong, whatever the explanation, if we have not heard from over half of the bears in man-world, there is a very grave problem. We'll talk to the adoption bears that are here directly. Go and seek out the ones who have arrived in the past octet of the yearling. Tell them we'll meet in the dining room at middle of the morrowmarch. We can then partake of the meal with them and question them, I hope, without arousing any fear. I can only presume that since none of them have come to any of the senior bears with concerns, they haven't yet seen the problem for themselves."

Beggrowgar, inclining his head towards William as an acknowledgement and a farewell, turned and left the study.

The meal

A twelfth of bears were gathered around one dining table. The fish stew was particular good this dayling. Wild salmon cooked with red berries and simmered in a ginger and caramel sauce. Yummy feasting that needed a repeat helping to fully appreciate the flavours. William and Beggrowgar, in spite of the seriousness of their mission, were also hungry diners revelling in the culinary skills of the kitchen bears.

"Thank you for coming to talk to us," began William. "We don't always get the chance to speak to you all when you arrive and in spite of everything that's going on at the moment with the light pillar, we thought it would be nice to catch up with you and to hear of your adventures in man-world."

"Yes," added Beggrowgar, "you must remember that we don't get the opportunity to live with humans anymore, so our only source of knowledge as to what is happening on a dayling basis is to talk to all of you."

"We're really happy to be having lunch with you today. Thanks for being here at short notice," William said, helping himself to a large portion of steamed treacle pudding. Quite where a bear of his size put the vast quantity of food he could eat at one sitting was a mystery to any bear who saw him dine.

"So, what can we tell you?" asked Lenny, an adoption bear who had only arrived at the castle a quintet of daylings earlier.

"Tell me about the life you have just finished. Did you enjoy it? I know all lives are different but was this one any different for any particular reasons?" William asked nonchalantly, trying to sound as if it was just general chit-chat.

"Well, in a way it was different because I didn't actually spend a lot of time with my owner, little Lucy, I spent most of the time with 'er father at his office," Lenny said and then belched loudly. Several of the other bears nodded approvingly. Belching was a compliment to the chefs and was expected after a good meal. "It did get a bit boring at times, but that's what Lucy wanted me to do."

Beggrowgar leaned forward, placed his forearms on the table and clasped his paws together. "That sounds a bit unusual. Didn't Lucy want you at home to play with her?"

"Nope she did buy me 'erself, from the charity shop, but she bought me as a present for 'er Dad. But I was 'er bear. I was born to 'er." Lenny chomped on a large piece of salmon from his stew and the senior bears waited, hind paws anxiously tapping beneath the table, for him to continue.

"See, she explained it to me when she got me 'ome. She gave me a cuddle, after 'er Mum made me go in the washing machine - ugh 'orrible that was and I didn't like that tumble dryer. Made me all itchy for days." Lenny shuddered at the memory.

"What happened after she cuddled you?" William encouraged, wanting to hear more about Lucy and less about Lenny.

"Lucy told me that 'er Dad worked in the office every day an' often at weekends. 'E was already on his way to work when she got up an' she was nearly always in bed by the time 'e got 'ome. Same during school 'olidays, although she stayed up later, but even then by the time 'e got 'ome and 'ad some dinner, 'e would fall asleep in the chair and Lucy was told to be quiet or go play upstairs in 'er room."

Several of the other bears sitting round the table agreed that their young owners had also had similar lives, especially in recent periods.

"But what has this got to do with Lucy buying you for her father? It would have made more sense for her to have you at home to play with if she was lonely," queried William.

Lenny was now eating his treacle pudding, having no difficulty alternating mouthfuls between sentences. It just made the narrative rather slow, much to William's irritation. But, being a kind bear he showed no sign of impatience and gently prodded Lenny to continue periodically. Several times during the telling Beggrowgar had an almost impossible to control urge to laugh, knowing full well the effect Lenny's eating would be having on the Lord High Bear. However, he too was a kind bear and did not want Lenny to be embarrassed, so with great self-control he suppressed the laughter. Unfortunately, that made him develop hiccups, so that he was the one who became embarrassed. Ellie, a little adoption bear sitting at the table with her brother, offered to fetch some water for Beggrowgar, who was slowly turning scarlet under his grizzled muzzle.

"Thank hc'p you hc'p," came the reply.

Lenny continued with his story. "Ah, but it wasn't so much that she was lonely, which she was a bit, but……that she thought 'er Dad didn't really care about 'er. 'E was always too busy or too tired to notice 'er. And, Lucy thought if 'e 'ad something at 'is office to remind 'im of 'er, then maybe, just sometimes, 'e would think of her and phone 'er, or tex' 'er or even come 'ome a bit earlier. That was to be my job, to make 'im think of 'er during the day."

"How very sad," said Beggrowgar, who had now recovered after drinking his water. "Did it work?"

"Well, luckily the next day, before Lucy sent me off with 'er father she did give me another big cuddle and a kiss, told me she loved me and she just knew I could do it. So with those magic words I was born again and I could make ‘er father think of ‘er while ‘e was at work. But it was very ‘ard work. At first I ‘ad to send out thoughts to all you ‘ere at the castle nearly every dayling for a spell that would make ‘im look at me and remember. After sometime you sent me spells that would last for a man-world week and that made it less tiring. But, even though I could get ‘im to look at me; I would move about overnight to a different place, sometimes on ‘is desk, sometimes on ‘is chair, sometimes on the filing cabinet, crafty eh! ‘E would come across me and be annoyed if I was in ‘is way, but it did make ‘im think of Lucy. If ‘e laughed ‘e would phone or tex’ ‘er, but lots of times ‘e would throw me out of the way and get on with ‘is work. I’d feel really sorry for Lucy on those days cos she would be waiting for a tex’ and nothing would be coming.”

Lenny wiped his muzzle with the back of his paw and licked carefully round his lips, hoping to find any small remaining morsel of pudding on his fur. “It’s very sad when people are too busy to remember their own children, even for just a few minutes. But that’s what it’s like out there now, everybody busy, busy, busy and yet not getting very far.” Lenny paused and all the other bears agreed. It was just like that. All the humans were either very, very busy or they did nothing.

“Nothing!” exclaimed William, putting down his spoon and looking at the bears who were all shaking their heads in agreement. "Nothing, what do you mean nothing?"

Sarah, a very pretty pink bear, looked at William with big, sad, oval eyes. "I was given to a young girl on her wedding day, a present from her new husband. At first, it was lovely, I would sit on her dressing table and watch her every morning when she arose and got ready for work." Sarah's tiny face crumpled, she looked down at the table and one large tear fell onto her empty plate. "But, after several months I gave up hope that she was ever going to cuddle me and say she loved me, so I had no chance of being born to her and carrying out my bear duties. It was very lonely." A large sigh escaped from her rose coloured mouth.

Beggrowgar was experiencing a very large warm empathy rising within and on leaving his chest he directed it across the table. The feeling surrounded the little pink bear and comforted her. "I am so sorry," said Beggrowgar, "but we still don't know what you all mean by nothing."

Sarah continued. "After the first year they both lost their jobs, the shop shut. That's when the nothingness started. For a little while they looked for other jobs, I could hear them talking about it, but gradually they stopped talking. They stayed in bed a lot longer and would just watch the big screen in the lounge. They would sit and eat take-aways. Gradually, Lorna - that was her name - ended up watching the big screen on her own. Her husband would stay in another room playing on the computer and talking to lots of other people on computers, but he never met them. They argued a lot and then it was all the time, then one day he just left. Lorna cried a lot, but then she got very angry and she threw all the things that had belonged to him, or that he'd given her, out into the dustbin ……..including me." Sarah's head dropped onto her thin furry arms and she sobbed.

Ellie climbed down from her chair and put her paws on Sarah's shoulders. "Don't cry anymore Sarah, you're safe now and you can stay here for as long as you need. I'll be your friend," and she patted the little pink bear's shoulder and nuzzled the top of the sobbing head.

"Oh deary, deary me," sighed William, scratching his left ear. "This is extremely sad and very worrying. I am most concerned," he looked across the table at the twin bears, who had not yet told their story. "And you duo? I am almost fearful to ask of you, is your story as bad?"

Ollie the slightly older of the pair, spoke first. "Oh please Lord High Bear, don't be despondent, not all the adoption bears have sad stories to tell. There are still a great many good owners in man-world, children and adults who truly love their bears and have them for many, many years; just like it always was. It is just that it has changed. Man-world has changed."

Ollie stopped and glanced at his sister, whom he loved dearly and had always tried to care for her in the bad times.

"Yes, that's so," added Ellie, who was remarkably just a smaller version of her brother.

"And your story, has your last life been a good one?" Beggrowgar enquired.

"Sadly, not really," Ellie whispered, looking at her brother to continue the tale.

"We belonged to a one yearling boychild and for the first two man years of his growth we all had a wonderful time. We were both born to him and he loved us dearly and included us in all his games. But by that time he'd been given so many cuddly toys and other bears that his head ran out of names for everyone. His room became crowded and the shelves were full. His mother slung a hammock across the ceiling and put us all in it. Joe couldn't reach any of us easily and would jump high from his bed and punch the hammock so that some of the toys would fall out and he could play with them. But because Joe had put Ellie and me in the hammock first, we were at the bottom and so couldn't fall out with all the other toys on top of us, so we never got played with anymore. We still tried to do our bear duties and we did send here for some spells asking for Joe to be happy."

William interrupted. "Do you not think the boy was happy with all his toys?"

"No," answered Ellie. "He had too many, all kinds, lots of war-game construction kits, hundreds of killing games to play on his own little screen machine." He would laugh loudly, get excited and jump up and down when he won one of these games, especially if he had been playing with his father or a school friend as he got older. But it didn't make him happy…. well, he was happy, for short times, but……..I think I mean content, it didn't make him content," Ellie finished.

"Yes, Ellie is right. We asked for spells to try and make him content and satisfied," added Ollie.

"Satisfied?" William asked.

"Mmmm, satisfied. You see he had so many things, it didn't matter if he broke anything because it just got replaced. So he didn't take care of anything and, even if things didn't break, after a few man-months they had to be got rid of anyway and replaced with updates. Joe was always asking his parents for updates of things. We didn't really understand for all these new things looked just the same as the old ones. We tried hard with the spells but eventually we stopped because they didn't help him. We'd been in the hammock for so long that I think our requests for spells were no longer reaching here. Without love we were not strong enough to send you our thoughts."

William slapped his head hard with his paw. Even with his thick fur the adoption bears could hear the thump and winced. "By the Great Grizzled One himself, I never knew it had got this bad. We must let the Grand Master know straight away. Come BG." William rose from the table, but then remembered the story was unfinished. "Ah, my friends please tell me, what happened in the end to Joe and you?"

"Eventually, Joe grew so tall that he would knock his head on the hammock, so he took it down. Most of the cuddly toys and bears he had never named were given to a charity shop. When he found us at the bottom of the pile, he did remember our names and laughed and actually gave us a hug. We liked that, it was like the Joe of old. He said he couldn't get rid of us so he tucked us away in the back of a drawer and there we stayed for many more years until Joe moved away from his parent's house and his mother found us. That's when we decided to come here; it had been so dark in the drawer for so long. We wanted to feel the sunshine again and talk with our own kind once more." Ellie finished sadly.

Beggrowgar looked at the quadful of bears who had endured such unfriendly lives and his vast kind heart was glad they had at last found sanctuary at the castle.

"We are very grateful to you all for sharing your stories with us. I am darkened that your tales could not have been more joyous, but please, enjoy your time here. Go and have some fun my young friends. Go down to the river and paddle or swim, for the water is still warm as the air is dried by the light, even though we have no sun."

William also smiled at them. "That's an excellent idea, go, enjoy, little cubs. And take your friends with you," he called out as the gaggle of bears sped away from the dining room back towards the west wing.

"Come BG we must hasten to Winkington and tell him of these grave events," William said in his deep gravelly voice.

Sitting in his large feather-down stuffed armchair Winkington had listened solemnly to William's recounting of the adoption bears stories. Now he stood and strolled to the Louis XIIIIth dresser. Taking down a trio of bone china mugs, he silently poured sweet hot tea into them. Placing them upon a solid silver salver that already held a plateful of gingernut biscuits, he offered the two bears the refreshment.

"I'm most grateful to you both for bringing me this information so quickly," Winkington said as he sank again into the well-worn armchair.

Beggrowgar offered apologies with regard to the discovery that they feared half the bears were not being born. "I cannot believe that we have been so unobservant in our duties and record-keeping Grand Master. I don't understand how it could have happened, I have no excuse, I can only say again how sorry I am."

Winkington put down his mug of tea and patted the upset bear on the paw. "Do not fret BG. This is no-one's fault. We have all been so busy and this place is usually one of happiness and enjoyment in our tasks. Maybe we have all become a shade complacent. The mistake, if there is one, has now been recognized and we can deal with it."

The sigh from Beggrowgar was one of relief and acceptance. He was truly a dutiful bear and the work carried out by him and William was always exemplary. In his heavy heart he knew no fault existed, he was just at a lost to know why he had not been more aware.

"William, it's now obvious that the adoption bears that are here at present have nearly all had very hard lives in man-world, for various reasons. They are also becoming much more aware that we senior bears are perturbed by the strange events concerning the light. They also know what happened to Rugle because they all saw his fall and, magnificently, they all helped with his recovery, using their own bodies to heat him." Winkington paced across the room and looked at the coat of arms above the fireplace.

"Servo Veneflicus," he read aloud, "Servo Veneflicus; 'Keep the Magic' that has always been our motto and creed my friends. We have always lived by Bear World's coat of arms and that is what we shall do now." Winkington swiveled round smiling to face the two puzzled bears who were wondering what the motto had to do with their present situation.

"The adoption bears come here to recuperate, have fun and as a reward for all their work while in man-world. We must ensure that this remains true even though our world here is under threat. We must keep the magic going for them. I will ask all you seniors to ensure that the routine of our cubs is interrupted as little as possible. From this dayling we will re-establish the story telling. Since the loss of the sun, very little activity has taken place outside and yet, as far as we know, there is no immediate danger. I will ask Aiggrowgar, who is very popular with the teddies, to tell one of his tales this morrowmarch." The Grand Master beamed at the now smiling duo, pleased with his decision.

"That is a splendid idea," William exclaimed delighted that this gathering, which had started so dismally was ending on an advantageous note. "The adoption bears have been staying in more of late. At our luncheon with them earlier we urged them to go play by the river. The more normality we can achieve the better the morale of every bear."

Chapter 8 AIGGROWGAR

The adoption bears were excited and gathering eagerly just beyond the path that led to the woods. Here in the meadow they sat in little groups, some directly on the lush grass, others on tartan rugs. A few of the more elderly ones lazed on the deck-chairs. Bears sprawled on their backs letting the arid air warm their round tummies, others preferred the face down resting on folded arms style. Two or three even played chase between the sitting bears and got a few 'tuts' when their exuberance and haste made them trip over spread out feet and paws. Gradually and without any real planning or thought a circle of bears formed, this was to be the story-teller's arena and today was the turn of the funniest of the Trusted Bears. His stories were legendary and not to be missed for in their abundance there was never time to repeat one.

A murmur weaved its way around the circle, he was on his way. Aiggrowgar strode along the track, arms swinging military fashion. Head erect, but slightly turned to the left, as his black eye-patch altered slightly his path of vision. No limp was noticeable today for he required respect, awe and wonder for his stories. The excited bears stopped their play, sat up straight, folded their arms or hugged their knees and waited for the great bear to arrive. Their anticipation grew as Aiggrowgar entered the circle carrying a long knarled stave.

"The dayling had been very long and busy and I was on my way back to this very castle." Aiggrowgar's voice beamed out, deep and full of resonance.

"I had been on a secret mission for the Grand Master, the safety of all the bears like you who lived here at that period, depended on my success. I had argued, discussed and persuaded all day to get an agreement with the Fearsome Hoveller."

The adoption bears gasped and startled back at the very name, although in all honesty, not one of them knew to whom the name referred or what type of creature it might be. Aiggrowgar spun round looking at them all, letting the name linger in the air for full effect.

"So, as I said I was on my way back with the scroll safely in my paw," he raised his paw above his head, "but I had a mighty thirst come upon me. Talking all day starts a dryness in the mouth that works its way over the tongue and down the throat, until the coughing seizures can't be stopped any further."

In unison all the bears nodded. "So, although I was on my way back, a short sojourn in the Grizzly Inn was well earned and I knew the Grand Master would expect me to quell my thirst. The inn was packed, a fresh catch of mackerel had been delivered from a sailing ship that very middle-day. The aroma of the smoking fish was just what I needed to help with the quantious supply of mead it takes to stop the coughing. With the scroll safely hidden under my rump fur I drank and ate, drank and talked, drank and……drank. A quintet of mead it took that nightling before the burning dryness went from my throat."

Aiggrowgar slowly revolved in the circle watching the bears to gauge their reaction. It was obvious the adoption bears were very, very, very impressed. This was never a quantity they would ever match.

"So, leaving the inn, I was on my way back to the castle, the scroll tucked securely in my belt," he patted his side, then shook the stick in front of him. "This very stave was the one I carried to make my travel through the woods clear of brambly obtrusions. It was now time of the night-dark and the sounds in the woods masked footfalls that otherwise I would have heard with these ears. Just where the path is lost and way must be made on uneven ground I was ATTACKED."

The gasp of the bears was loud and several covered their eyes in fright. Aiggrowgar leaped into the air waving the stave and gave a deep throttled growl. Some bears now quickly moved their paws from their eyes and covered their ears instead.

"I leapt and roared, I hit out with my stave. I thrust left, right and middling, high and low, but the two ragamuffins, for indeed it was they, had taken me by surprise and I fell crashing to the ground. But, did I give up? Never. I continued to roar and shout and guard the scroll. The ragamuffins grew weary and ran off without the scroll. The Fearsome Hoveller would have made them pay for their failure the next morrowmarch, for it must have been he who had sent them. No-one else would have dared intrude upon me, Aiggrowgar, the first of the Trusted Bears.

Weary and bruised, I scrambled to my feet and hastily started once more on my way to the castle.... albeit, a bit confused and light of the head. It was near night-grey when I emerged along the path yonder. Lord Montgomery - Bearmont was walking my way. He had become anxious at my long absence and sought for sign of me. Whatever has happened to you he asked hurrying forward to reach me. I've been attacked by four ragamuffins in the woods, I explained. Quickly, we must get you safely in the castle and he helped me along. At the gate William was waiting he had seen our approach from the library window. Goodness me, you are a state Aiggrowgar he said and I explained that eight raggas had set upon me. William asked Bearmont to sit me in the kitchen while he would go and fetch Duggrowsar.

It was still only dawnling when I sat at the big table and one of the adoption bears scurried to bring me some hot, sweet porridge. They would never have got me down if there had not been a dozen of them I growled as the bowl was placed in front of me. I began to sup but the porridge was harsh hot against my gashed muzzle. OOOOH I yelled, I will get my revenge against that score of ragamuffins."

The bears listened enthralled their eyes wide, breath held as Aiggrowgar continued with his tale and the somewhat growing band of marauders who had attacked him.

"Duggrowsar came into the kitchen with William. She carried some potions and some hot towels. The towels she wound around my chest and the potions she applied to the many bruises. I think you have had a lucky escape really Aiggrowgar, nothing too serious. Huh, it will take more than two score of them raggeties to beat me I claimed.

By now the kitchen was full of bears coming to have breakfast and coming to hear the wondrous tale of my escape. I leapt upon the table and showed them how I had fought off the murderous rabble, turning this way and that and swinging my stave around my head.

Suddenly the kitchen hushed and I spun round and saw the Grand Master had entered the room. Climbing down from the table, I recounted my adventure to him. How many raggeties Aiggrowgar he asked. With paw on my chest," the old warrior demonstrated this action, "I said loudly two score and four came forth from the bushes Grand Master, but I still have the scroll. I produced it with a flourish from my belt and handed it to him with a bow.

Good he said I am pleased that no real harm has befallen you. What do you propose to do about this army of bandits, if anything, he asked me smiling. I thought and thought a bit more. I shall go back to town when recovered and seek vengeance. Winkington asked me to be careful, but nothing would have stopped me. So a trio of morrows later, I returned at night-dark to the very inn I had frequented on that fateful night. It had been brought to me on the wind that the ragamuffins were there each nightling boasting of what they'd done. I sat quietly in the shadows, hidden in my cloak waiting for them to reach the topsy state of mead and then fall, snoring. It was a twice of time before all two score and four snored loudly on the benches, their heads too heavy for their scrawny necks and so they lay across the tables."

Aiggrowgar again leapt into the air with a war-cry startling the bears listening to him so intently.

"Like a lightning bolt I grabbed a brace of them at a time and head-first stuffed them into empty fish barrels from the cellar. Then I sealed the lids with honeycomb and in a line I rolled those barrels out the door, along the cobbles, to the very edge of the cliff and.... tipped them over. Except for one.

So, once more, I was on my way back to the castle with that one barrel containing the very first brace of ragamuffins that had emerged that night. I rolled them all the way kicking them along with my great padded feet and they screamed and yelled and begged to be let out all the way here." Aiggrowgar acted out this last piece of the story with kicking actions all around the circle, so that the bears could see the size of his feet and wonder at their strength.

"I unstopped the barrel at the feet of Winkington and the duo tumbled out, a sorry brace, shamefaced and scared. I asked the Grand Master what would be their fate. He answered straight away, enquiring first what I had done with the other two score and two. The sea has them, I growled, where they will bob along for many morrows. Winkington, wise as ever, decreed that these two, being the primary raggas, would spend as long as it took to dig out a new bigger, warmer, brighter cave for Rugle. This was a fit punishment and I was satisfied that some useful thing would come from this misdeed. The ragamuffins were petrified of Rugle and spent a twelfth of times each morrow for the next quad of years digging the cave; anytime they stopped the dragon would roar his fire at their pointed toes and they would dance on the hot ground until exhausted." Aiggrowgar stopped speaking, looked all around and folded his arms.

The adopted bears waited to see if this was the end of the story and with no more forthcoming Scruff asked, "What happened to the barrels, did anyone ever see them again?"

Aiggrowgar smiled at the tubby bear, "No my friend, the barrels bobbed along for however long it took to reach a forgotten island far away to sea. There they splayed out onto the sand and the ragamuffins live to this day. Nor can they ever come back for none know the way."

"And the duo who dug Rugle's cave, where did they go?" asked Rachel.

Aiggrowgar turned to face from where the query emanated, smiled and with a shrug of his broad shoulders replied, "Ah, my pretty one, for that answer you will have to ask Rugle."

With his fine tale ended and the thought of Rugle

with the ragamuffins Aiggrowgar began to laugh ....the adoption bears with wondrous eyes watched to see if this was to be one of those that become legend.

The laugh started in Aiggrowgar's belly, it chuckled upwards to his heaving chest; it chortled and hurtled into his throat. His mouth opened, the rows of teeth bared, his nostrils glistened as the laugh hurled outwards becoming thunderous as it met the air. All the teddies that had been in the circle curled tightly into little balls, making themselves as small and as low as it is possible for a bear to be. The new ones automatically copied the few experienced bears who had lived through one of Aiggrowgar's laughs before. They knew with just a slight piece of luck, the laugh would carry high into the air as Aiggrowgar tossed back his head. Thus would they escape the primary, most damaging vibrations and live to see another day!!

The bears inside the castle stopped, listened and, as one, scuttled to the corridors to find the nearest guffaw bar and so secure a safe hold. They clung on in ones, duos and in places trios in their haste to be prepared. Some bears faced the coming onslaught, hind legs firmly stanced on the floor. Others braced with their backs against the now descending guffaw. As the warm living breath swooshed against them their fur flattened, their lips grimaced and their cheeks shook on their closed eye faces.

Micky, an adoption bear who was the last in line of a trio, found his feet lifting from the ground, his hind paws sliding upwards until he was horizontal along the wall. He clung on desperately, his front paws locked together around the bar.

Curly Ken, who had been too short to reach a bar and had not experienced an Aiggrowgar guffaw before, tumbled backward somersaults along the lengthy corridor before he finally came to rest beside the great door of the kitchen. He quickly decided the best way to restore his equilibrium would be to eat a huge bowl of steaming porridge and he scuttled on all fours into the sanctuary of the welcoming kitchen.

The quietening guffaw swooshed finally through the cave, making music as it slowed through Rugle's scales, at last reaching the sea creating waves that would ripple outwards for a trio of leagues.

Afterwards, everyone agreed it had been a magical story and it would become a legendary laugh, but perhaps they all needed a rest before the next one.

Chapter 9 THE PREPARATION

Eaggrowgar and Duggrowsar, following their meeting with the Grand Master, decided to make their way to the library and see what knowledge was available. With the help of William, they wanted to discover anything that would help in the fight against the light column.

The two bears made themselves comfortable, choosing two big soft armchairs by one of the large windows in the Spell-room.

"Tell me more of your thoughts Dooey. This dragon thing, can you explain a bit more please?"

Duggrowsar clasped her paws together, automatically examining the gold nail-varnish for chips as she did so, then leaning well back in the armchair she let out a long sigh. "I wish I could be more certain, all of this is only conjecture, but what else do we have? I do believe that Winkington is right though. We are under attack from all the bad thoughts and traits of mankind, they've built up over time to a point where all the negative energies have come together to form a power, a sort of energy hub, much the same as the old Chinese master suggested. I believe the column has become a light dragon. That's why it attacked Rugle, it saw him as the good dragon."

Eaggrowgar had listened intently but was still puzzled. "I understand the energy bit, but a dragon! How can it transform into a dragon, or anything else for that matter?"

"It needs an identity to be able to operate......to be able to attack. I'm certain that it has adopted a dragon's format and so we must see it as such and retaliate as if it is a real dragon that we are fighting. And we have to fight it on both levels, one as a dragon and the other as energy."

Still Eaggrowgar persisted in his effort to understand. "But why a dragon of all things?" He frowned, "Although of course that makes it fierce and frightening to face."

"You're right there," Duggrowsar smiled back, "the only thing I can think of is that the first thing the light encountered as a possible attack upon itself was Rugle. It therefore adopted the same form. It created within itself an identity to match and fight what it saw as a threat. Remember, it sucked Rugle's heat, his fuel. Maybe it used it to create its own persona."

Eaggrowgar let out a sound – half whistle, half sigh. "Wow Dooey, that's frightening. It really is a living entity then. I'm not sure if I think that makes it easier to fight or harder!"

"I know, but in some way it must be easier to fight something we can actually see..... isn't it?"

The golden haired bear leaned forward in his chair and looked directly at his friend. "Did you know I was with Isaac Newton in the mid 1600's? He was very interested in the work of the English physicists Boyle and Hooke. They'd written about the refraction of light by using a glass prism. I'm now wondering if their work could help us in our fight."

Eaggrowgar now sounded enthusiastic and his thoughts began to tumble from his brain quicker than he could convert them to words. "There's also a French philosopher and scientist by the name of Rene Descartes who did a large amount of research into light. Check if William has any info on these people and I'll refresh myself with the work of Newton. Meet back in a duo cycle?"

"Hold on Dooey," William cried. "Slow down a bit, please." Duggrowsar was bombarding him with so many questions that he was, at first, unsure of her priorities. Once he had these established, he helped all he could in guiding her to the relevant parts of the library.

Duggrowsar ploughed through books, manuscripts and documents, looking for clues that might help. In her search she came across a Feng Shui book and noted, with interest, that the Chinese year at the beginning of the 20th century had been the year of the Dragon. The more the bearess read and researched, the more convinced she became of the immense power of light when harnessed. The light column was far from just a simple element.

The pair met up after the middling as arranged. Duggrowsar was the first to speak.

"I'm beginning to realise that there's a lot of significance in Lexington's remarks about the centre tower being the heart of the castle. If I can explain, there's the physical heart; concerned with living and survival and the spiritual heart; the power to love, to care and sadly, to hurt. I'm sure the light has taken on the facade of a dragon, as it needs the identity to enable it to have a heart. Just as it chose a dragon's form when it encountered Rugle, so it needs a heart to fight the castle's heart, the symbol of all that is good in Bear World." She watched the large bear's face to see what impact her words were having.

The scientist showed little, if any, surprise. Having accepted that the light was a living thing, he had also come to the same overall conclusion.

"So now we need to decide how to fight back and destroy both parts of this thing," he replied simply. "And, as the old saying says, one destroys like with like. Reflectors are the answer!"

They spent what seemed like an entire cycle talking of ways to fight back, ways to defend and who was to do what. They considered what they had learnt in lives past and tried to decide whether any of it was relevant to their present situation. In between the discussions they were fortified with spicy fruit cakes washed down with lemon and honey tea. Sarah, the little pink adoption bear, had come into the library to find a book to read. Seeing how busy the duo of Trusted Bears were and hearing from William that they had been there most of the dayling, her kind heart and eagerness to help had allowed her to appoint herself chief food-fetcher. William was warmed as he watched the little bear humming to herself as she padded back and forth from the kitchen to the library and he thought again, as he had numerous times over the centuries, how fortunate he was to live at Wynghorran and meet so many wonderful bears.

"OK," said Eaggrowgar, rising from his chair and stretching his legs, "at last we have a plan! It's the only one we have, so we'll have to assume its right."

"Sounds good to me," encouraged Duggrowsar, wriggling her shoulders to ease the cramp that had developed unnoticed while she worked. "Let's go see Winkington."

Decisions

The Grand Master had called all the senior bears together in the rest-room of the central tower. This plan was going to involve every bear living at the castle. A feat never before attempted, but this was a fight to save Bear World and all of their lives.

Duggrowsar and Eaggrowgar stood side by side eager, but nervous, to explain their findings and how they planned to move forward. Winkington had already explained that they had devised a plan that he supported and believed had a good chance of success.

"As with any battle there are risks, but risks we must accept. I have met with Rugle and he will join with us in our fight," he concluded.

Duggrowsar detailed how she and Eaggrowgar had arrived at the formulation of the plan; why they believed the light had evolved into a dragon and how they meant to defeat it.

"We will need the help of Rugle, for once we destroy the column itself, the dragon within will be set free to attack the castle direct. We have plans to support Rugle that we'll come to later." Duggrowsar paused, shuffled her feet a little, glanced down at her notes and then continued.

"As I've just said, we must first defeat the column, and that won't be easy. We must attack the column by reflection. Reflect back its own energy; in effect get it to eat itself." She paused again, to see if anyone was going to question what had been said so far. All the bears were concentrating on her words intently, not one would have had the discourtesy to interrupt. Neither did they have any queries, for they had all, daylings previously, stopped being astonished at anything being said about the light.

"If we can get that far, the column will evaporate releasing the light dragon and that is when Rugle will start his attack. We will then all be working together to defeat the dragon and support Rugle."

Eaggrowgar stepped forward. "There is another challenge that we face, we believe that the centre tower here has acted as an aerial, attracting the light. And, our ancient clock up there is like its ticking heart. The tower is the most obvious place for the dragon to attack first, but as the highest point we want to have bears upon its roof. We've discussed with Winkington duties for the battle." He turned towards the Grand Master asking, "OK if I go ahead and explain?"

"Please do."

Eaggrowgar continued, "Winkington will obviously be Battle Commander with overall responsibility for communications and orders. Bearmont and AG, you will bear the centre tower from its parapet. As said, it's the highest point of the castle and so will give you an advantage with the column destruction and when we need to feed Rugle with heat from the sun. You might well be the first to catch the sun's rays as there will be no impediment because of the height. We feel that....."

This time there was an interruption. From the Major, "Sun? We don't have any sun."

Duggrowsar interjected, "Quite right Bearmont, but we expect the sun to reappear immediately the light column is dissipated."

Nodding in agreement, Eaggrowgar continued, "We feel that Rugle's very life will depend on us being able to keep him fed with heat, so that he doesn't run out of fuel, or have it sucked from him as happened before. The reflectors we make have a duo purpose, to destroy the column, as already outlined and to aid Rugle."

"That's a lot of guesswork and a lot of supposing." Aiggrowgar commented glaring at the speaker. "Are we certain of anything?"

Winkington, sensing that not all the bears were being convinced, especially, surprisingly, the more experienced battle bears, stepped in. He quickly realised that fighting this new type of enemy, one that couldn't be identified or attacked conventionally was unsettling for the old warriors. "I understand your concerns completely. This is a new situation for us all. The most we can do is give it our best guess. Plan as much as we can and the most important thing of all is to be prepared that nothing may go as described and we must be ready to adapt. All this you can do." The great bear surveyed his comrades and then spoke slowly with a conviction that could be heard in every syllable. "You ask are we certain of anything. Yes my friends I am, I have faith in every one of you. We will succeed, of that I am certain." The senior bears were heartened and reassured by the Grand Master's words. As he looked at the row of nodding heads, Winkington silently wished he could have managed to reassure himself as easily.

Eaggrowgar focused his attention on Bearmont and Aiggrowgar once more. "You will need to take under your command a score of adoption and castle bears. We expect the light dragon, on his release, to go directly for the centre tower. He will see that Rugle is in the air waiting for him, so hope to get in his first blow a.s.a.p. Your bears will have to stand fast as the light dragon will come in at full speed with all the flame, or whatever it is he uses, he can throw at us."

"Our bears will stand fast under battle, they are brave little cubs and will do whatever we ask of them and more," Aiggrowgar growled.

"I know, I know. Will you also please spend time with Rugle and give him some of your expertise on battle tactics," Eaggrowgar replied trying to appease the old warrior. "Ideas on how best to gain advantage when he is in the air battling the light dragon. You might want to work out some basic tactics that will allow you to anticipate his next move."

Growling again Aiggrowgar said, "He's a dragon, he will have fought most of his battles in the air. I'm sure he doesn't need me to tell him how to gain advantage up there." Realising that he may be sounding slightly peeved at having a scientist tell him how to fight he added, "But of course working out a few moves would be useful."

With some degree of relief Eaggrowgar next spoke to William and Beggrowgar, not noticing that after the exchange with the old warrior he switched the first two words of his sentence and changed his command into a request. "Will you be responsible for the training. Half the bears will learn how to use the reflector. But before we can get them to you we would like you to train your half in drill, section movement, hand signals, etc. and choose some section commanders. The other half of the bears will be engaged in the manufacture of the reflector."

Duggrowsar now took up the instructions once more, "Lex and CG you will oversee and manage the manufacturing of the reflectors. Each bear will make two, they will have to select a partner before they start because we need to build a trio of sizes small, medium and large and each bear will need to know what size to make for his partner. If they can pair in similar sizes it will be easier to organise and manage when the battle starts. The pairs can then teach their partners what they have learnt. That's the general instructions, the rest; the specifics are probably best done in groups, according to what part you are now in charge of. As for ourselves, Eaggrowgar will be battle co-ordinator and support Winkington in any fallen Trusted Bear replacement. I will be medical support but mainly after the battle, unless absolutely vital, as my position will be on the fore-shore dug in with a group of cubs." All the bears present, except for the one concerned, recognised the 'absolutely vital' referred to the Grand Master. The only bear who was not expendable.

The wily herbalist then beamed at the male bears, "Thank you for your patience, I know we've given you a lot to think about and an awful lot to do, but can I just say, if I have to go into battle then I am just so grateful that it is with all of you. I know I and all the cubs are as safe as we can possibly be. Thank you."

Winkington chuckled to himself as he watched all his friends standing erect and puffing out their hairy chests at Duggrowsar's words. Appointing a girl as a Trusted Bear had been one of his better decisions, although that had not been a consideration at the time. "I also thank you. We have much to do, let us take the remainder of this dayling to plan, the next morrowmarch to train and manufacture and on the trio – we battle."

The bears broke into groups. Eaggrowgar gave his drawings of the reflector to Lexington. “I need you to turn my outline specifications into reality and make them work Lex. Is it possible?”

“No reason why not. We just have to get the angles correct and make them easy to turnover.” Lexington examined the drawings and scrutinised the scribbled notes alongside the sketches. “Yep, reckon that can be done. The umbrella will reflect the light and the sun’s rays alright, but I can’t guarantee the success of the scheme though!” The duo, twisting the drawings this way and that, continued their discussions. After half a cycle Lexington suggested, “Tell you what, let’s meet up with CG and Woodrow in the main workshop to discuss the design and how we are going to manufacture these umbrellas of yours in more detail.”

Duggrowsar, William, Beggrowgar and Bearmont sat at one of the octagonal tables in the rest room, thus leaving themselves with plenty of space to take notes and draw plans. The tables were more normally employed in holding jig-saws and sketch-pads, or board games and cards. For a table to be bereft of craft equipment was a rarity. Glue, scissors, ribbons and beads, remnants from an earlier dweller, adorned the table next to the one they now occupied.

"Thank you for coming Bearmont, we need your experience. With such little time to train our bears in military manoeuvres and discipline, you and Aiggrowgar are invaluable to us. Would you like to start off?"

Feeling at last, that here was something he could get his very large teeth into, the Major spent the next duo of the cycle happily outlining basic training, its importance and how to command on a battlefield.

"So you see," Lexington was explaining to Woodrow, the manager as well as being the chief carpenter, of the workshops. "It's imperative that we get the angles and reflective material correct so that we can catch the light and the sun and direct it precisely where we want it to go. We also need to make sure that the umbrellas can be turned, sighted and aimed quickly. They must not be too heavy or our cubs will not be able to hold them steady."

He then picked up a sample of sailcloth, lying on the nearest bench and passed it to Coggrowgar, stretching up in an effort to reach the much taller, heavier bear. "CG, here's where your expertise comes in. We need a framework on which to attach the reflective material, tinfoil will be the easiest, but the outside of the umbrella will look fairly ordinary."

Coggrowgar had been studying the design and had already decided how to cut and sew the covering. He had tracked down some bales of cloth and the sample Lexington handed to him was the one he had made earlier, as a trial, while the architect was busy with Woodrow. He produced a belly laugh that ruffled his fur as if a gentle breeze was passing through him.

"Not a problem my little friend. Leave it to me."

The work shop section managers were involved in getting the tooling and the raw materials ready. Woodrow discussed with them how they could organise and work with small groups of bears when the manufacturing started. A test bed was also needed to ensure the sights worked correctly and were easy to use. There was excitement, mixed with apprehension, at all the activity and the workshop rumbled with the sound of bears working.

Aiggrowgar climbed down to the fore-shore in search of Rugle. He lumbered along the beach with an uneven gait; with his limp sand was not an easy surface to walk on. The dragon was fishing in the shallows, spearing his favourite food with the cruel looking talons. Watching him, Aiggrowgar was glad that Rugle was his friend but admitted to himself not for the first time that dayling, that the coming battle between a pair of dragons would be a glorious spectacle to behold. A once in all lifetimes spectacular. A moment of shame overtook him when he thought of what had befallen Rugle last time, but he knew there was no malice in his thoughts; it was just a visual image about watching a magnificent beast in battle.

Rugle waded from the sea, shook himself and hailed the approaching honey-coloured bear. "What brings you here at this time friend?" he called.

"Been sent to tell you how to fight!" came the reply. Aiggrowgar sat on the rock and observed the dragon gracefully fold his tail and wings into his body, to make himself as small as possible. He lowered his neck until he was level with the bear and together they burst into laughter.

"Oh dear," snorted Rugle, "what words of wisdom are you about to impart?"

"None whatsoever. I've done well to hold my temper today. I've also been told how to plan a battle." He lifted his eye patch and wiped away the sweat with his paw. "I'm getting old and crotchety Rugle, not got the patience I used to have. I shouldn't be taking it out on my closest friends. They'd worked so hard to produce their battle plans......and actually they were very good."

Rugle shared his fish with Aiggrowgar. "No harm done, I'm sure they are as aware as you of the strain everyone is under. No wonder tempers are a spot frayed, natural dear fellow, natural."

"You're right. Anyway now I'm here is there anything I can do or we can discuss that might help.

Having a few tricks up our claws could tip the balance in our favour......if we need it of course."

"Quite right, come into the cave, it will soon be night-grey and getting a bit chilly for my scales. I have a very good barrel of Devon cider waiting to be shared. Let's go talk tactics."

Bear World Coat of Arms

Chapter 10 TRAINING DAY

The training of so many bears was not going to be an easy task but, as always, they were willing to please. Duty was inbuilt and a component of bear genes. The cubs loved excitement and being involved in anything new. If curiosity was also a gene, it was a very large one. The cubs had picked their partners, some were friends or at least knew each other, others found themselves partnered with bears simply because of size. The cubs formed into a duo of groups. The chatter was noisy with the asking and comments about the coming training. Order was called and the bears went higgley-piggley to their respective training areas.

The designated manufacturers skipped, leapt and tumbled to the main workshop squashing themselves in until the floor could no longer be seen beneath the plethora of padded furry feet. They sat beneath and upon benches. They squatted on the wood-work machinery and flattened themselves against the industrial size sewing machines, trying to avoid the treadles as Woodrow explained the plan. The cubs would work in small groups after collecting the raw materials under the guidance of the supervisors and the pair of Trusted Bears in charge of operations; Lexington and Coggrowgar. Each cub was to make a duo of reflectors, one for themselves and one for their partners. The atmosphere was still one of general excitement, but now concern for the coming battle and learning to master the new weapon, diluted their gaiety.

One of the adoption bears Jamie, a new cub to the castle and one who, sadly, had not been born in his previous life in man-world was a little lost. He had lived with a very rich family but had not been loved, he was just a trophy displayed on a shelf but never cuddled. He had not yet had time to make any friends or even acquaintances, but he was an intelligent bear and keen to impress. Jamie found himself in the first queue, the wire and cane stores. The supervisor when he saw Jamie at the stores desk, roared to the stores foreman.

"Duo kits size small for this young cub Fred."

“Thank you sir,” Jamie responded, giving a salute as he collected the framework.

The supervisor stopped, looked up from his check-list and rubbed his muzzle. That one will get on, he thought to himself and then reverted his attention to the next bear in line. The cubs collected their equipment from a thrice of stores before making their way to the assembly area. The clip and press machines proved the hardest for the cubs to master but Coggrowgar noticed one bear became competent quickly and was soon showing some of the more hesitant oncs how to do it.

“Well done young cubling, good work. You are?”

“Jamie,” answered the young bear.

The other half of the cubs was practising drill training. This is going to be more of a challenge for us than first envisaged thought the Major. As one of the most experienced military bears he had already given the bemused cubs his introductory ‘soldiers-at-arm and the world of battles’ short lecture. The marching drill and the learning how to use the reflector practice had all gone to plan. Except for Lady Linda. No way, try as she did again and again could she keep in step with the others.

“Tick-tocking,” growled Bearmont, “that’s what we used to call it.” He was explaining the condition to William and Beggrowgar. “Means the recruit can’t get the arms and legs to work together. They thrust forward an arm and a leg on the same side of the body, instead of opposites. Hardest thing in the world to correct," he mumbled.

Aiggrowgar was walking past and watched the puzzled William and Beggrowgar staring at the Major marching up and down demonstrating the problem.

"Ha-ha, got a tick-tock in the ranks my Old Pup?" He roared, "Give 'em to me. I'll sort it in a quart." He escorted Lady Linda into the garden. A duo before the middling time, a sheepish looking Aiggrowgar returned alone.

"She seems very intelligent, perhaps we could make her a radio operator," he suggested to William. At that moment, Lady Linda emerged from the garden with a squeal of delight.

"I did it, I did it," she shouted marching towards them correctly. The senior bears grinned at Linda and at each other.

"Well done," shouted Bearmont as the female bear in her excitement speeded up, tripped over her left hind paw and fell into Beggrowgar's outstretched arms.

After that the dayling passed without further incident and just before the night-grey the well trained bears marched back to the west wing for dinner.

“I bet,” began Winkington, “that our great little cubs will be having an early night, but my guess is that they won’t be sleeping easily.”

Chapter 11 THE NIGHT-DARK

The senior bears were all ensconced in their own rooms for the length of the night-dark. Each one was restless, without sleep and without their bed. Each pondered on what the morrowmarch might bring - the time of the battle. Each had their own fears, hopes and mindset on the possible outcome. Each aimed for victory, but none, unknown to each other, felt certain it would be claimed.

Major Montgomery had finished his castle reconnaissance at the ending of the night-grey. Nothing stirred and it would have been pointless to continue patrols throughout the remaining hours. He needed to be alert and rested for the coming battle. But rested he was not. Having paced the room in every circle and direction possible he now occupied the window seat from where he could see the light. His gaze rested on the ever-revolving column. Bearmont had battled across time and space, being a veteran of many campaigns, but never had he encountered a foe like this one. What are you he pondered? Why are you here? What do you hope to achieve? He now considered the column to have a conscience and so now gave it bear attributes to think and plan. He sipped periodically at the very large hot milk and brandy he had poured himself in an attempt to encourage sleep. In spite of Winkington's affirmations, inside Bearmont felt he had failed in his duty to protect the castle and its occupants. He believed his two attempts to fight the light should at the very least have resulted in weakening it, but nothing tangible had been achieved. Give me something solid to fight he silently asked. Something I can attack, something that will bleed. Something that will die. The battle plan was firmly established in his head. He could find no flaws in its structure and yet he had no idea if it would succeed. Finishing the hot toddy he reluctantly lumbered to his bed, climbed in, pulled the rough woollen blanket over his head and ordered himself to sleep. Allowing himself to get exhausted would be a dereliction of duty in the Major's military world.

Beggrowgar was also looking at the light column from his window. He was a duo of layers above the Major's quarters, but occupied the same position in the north wing. Unbeknown, his sturdy hind paws had many times that nightling traced the same patterns being padded out below. The eager bear had first learnt from his tuition in Persia that answers to most things could be found in a book. All a bear had to do was find the right book. The Royal trader, for whom he had worked in those past centuries, could locate a book and an answer to any question within the tripling of a blink. His work when stocking the library and with William had confirmed Beggrowgar's belief in this theory. So it was that for the past trio of the cycle the tubby bear had searched, examined and skimmed through his own collection of works upon the sundry bookshelves that adorned all walls in the pentagon shaped room. His life experience, like the other senior bears, had not prepared him for this new enigma. He believed that somewhere there must be a reference to the light. It could surely not be a unique phenomenon. It must have occurred before, somewhere, sometime, he reasoned. But all his references had led nowhere. He was anxious about the coming morrow for he was not like some, a warrior, neither was he a fighter. He had no experience of battle. His strength was in encouragement, in organisation, in doing practical tasks. His unstinting efforts in training the adopted bears, alongside William, to use the reflectors had been noted by the Grand Master himself. With the fresh dayling he would be tasked with leading a group of bears to be in the right place at the right time. He dearly wished and aimed to fulfil this task, he knew it to be within his capabilities, but yet the night-dark brought doubts and allowed to rise the bleak thoughts that one could be found wanting. With a large sigh and a shaking of his shoulders to rid them of tension,

Beggrowgar closed the volume of books before him and finally retired to his goose-feathered bed.

Lexington was checking the reflector angles for the ninth time since reaching his chamber. Re-measuring meticulously with protractor and compass he could find no fault with his earlier calculations. It will work, it must work, he repeatedly told himself. As long as I have calculated the angles correctly, we can redirect as necessary. He repeated the mantra in his mind until he convinced himself that success would be achieved. Carefully rolling his diagrams and drawings he replaced them into the wide bamboo tubes and stood them alongside the wall by his bed. Being able to see them in the night when he woke would be re-assuring. I have built castles, fortresses, pyramids, mazes, even crystal palaces, Lexington told himself; surely to grizzlies I am capable of building a legion of umbrellas! With that thought the small bear smiled at his own self-doubt and decided it was time to retire to his very inviting bed.

Coggrowgar had worked all dayling non-stop alongside the work-shop and adoption bears to manufacture the reflectors. One of the biggest bears at the castle, his back now ached from the bending and stooping that had accompanied his efforts of helping the others to build the reflectors. His paws were stiff from the cutting and sewing of the cloth for the umbrellas. He grimaced as he flexed his claws, straightening them with some difficulty. So much for all those years I spent making and mending sails, he thought. I must be getting old, I have the skills still, but not the dexterity. He backed against the heavy oak upright beam that took pride of place in the centre of his quarters and rubbed his back, side to side, up and down; scratching and massaging the weary muscles. His thoughts focused on the coming morrowmarch and he was impatient for its arrival. Taking command, making instant decisions, gaining supremacy against the elements these were the things that made his blood flow fast and hot. After all what is this light if not elements, he rationalised. The old sea-captain was ready to sail into battle again. He swung himself up into his bunk humming an old sea shanty that had been a favourite of Nelson's.

William was practicing turning his reflector upside-down, timing his action. It was not just a matter of how fast he could do it, his concern was how fast all the bears could do it. Co-ordination was going to be the key to their success. For a twelfth of the cycle he and Beggrowgar had trained the adoption and castle bears to master the skill so they could act as one. He had thought that learning to turn the umbrella and line up the sights was difficult enough, trying to do it as one unit was almost asking too much of the bears. What splendid cubs we have, William thought proudly, remembering their eagerness to please and their tenacity. He had been fascinated by the idea of using reflectors and would deeply have loved to have been able to use mirrors. He mused on his idea of a mosaic of glass pieces and drew an alternative reflector design for his own amusement. Sad glass weighs so heavily, he thought. As usual sleep did not descend readily on William and his attention turned upon his telescope. He scoured the skies seeking any unfamiliar pattern in the constellations that might, just might give an explanation for the appearance of the light at this particular time.

Duggrowsar was pleased with her preparations. She had worked tirelessly all the night-grey grinding and blending, with her pestle and mortar, the herbs and spices she might have need of on the morrowmarch. She looked at the labelled glass bottles with the cork lids neatly arranged alphabetically on the table. That is more than enough to suffice, she thought, hoping in reality that there would be no cause for their use. Making the medicines soothed her, in the familiarity of the routine she was reassured and comforted that all would be well and life would be in control again.

She had been delighted that middle-dayling to receive a consignment of fresh turmeric from her close friend and mentor Merganza. Turmeric used as a poultice was still the best way she knew to treat a wound, especially if it had become septic. Thinking of

Merganza, brought her wish to visit the remarkable, ginger tufted bear to the front of her mind. Duggrowsar longed to see the knot garden, filled with herbs that her friend had designed and described in great detail. Merganza had been born to the prince when he was a toddler and she was still greatly loved. At Highgrove she lived on the royal bedside cabinet and slowly and quietly, over many man-years, she had transferred her knowledge into the sleeping prince's thoughts. He had planted the knot garden exactly as she had envisaged. Many happy hours had been spent by the prince and the bear tending to the herbs.

Perhaps I am just a micro envious at times of such a beautiful garden Duggrowsar thought. But she was justifiably proud of her own achievements at Wynghorran and spent a quadling of the cycles tending her own herb garden. Sometimes one or two adoption bears would show an interest in her work and then she would impart recipes to the teddies and make spice cakes with them in the great kitchen so that they could share them with friends.

She glanced once more at the laden table as she finished her lemongrass tea and was satisfied. Duggrowsar removed her mascara, washed her face, cleaned her sharp teeth and slipped gracefully under the white silk duvet.

Eaggrowgar being a scientist and mathematician could easily compartmentalise his activities and thoughts. His dayling work being complete he was now allaying any doubts that could enter a resting mind, by picking a particularly difficult piece to play on his cello. To play music was his way of relaxing. His composing skills were recognized throughout Bear World and he had been commanded to play for Kings, the famous and the infamous. He had been part of the quartet who had first played Beethoven's now famous cantabile melody, the beautiful Pathetique Sonata- Adagio. Sometimes Eaggrowgar gave lessons here at the castle and his recitals were just as popular with the adoption bears as was the story-telling.

His soulful music drifted through the window and was heard by Lexington as he lay in bed gazing at the bamboo tubes. William also caught the melody on the wind as he searched the stars. Pleased with his performance, not a single note had been missed or wrongly struck; Eaggrowgar placed the cello in its leather case and retired to bed.

Aiggrowgar was preparing to be immaculate in his appearance for the morrowmarch. He wanted to be 'shipshape and battle-fashion', ready to lead the bears in the fight against the light. Although pleased to have been selected to be at the top of the clock tower with Bearmont, as this would be the primary line of defence, he also thought no other bear could have filled the role. Who else could possibly lead the task he thought, there is only me and the Old Pup that's capable of doing it. He had earlier walked in the orchard and, with his heavy axe, chopped a strong, young branch to make a new stave. Experience had taught him first class equipment was vital for success. As he drank the hot water laced with mead, he whittled a handle for the stave in the shape of a bear's head. He peered intently with his good eye at his progress and surprised himself at the intricacy of the design. That'll impress 'em he thought.

Aiggrowgar was a doer, not a thinker. A practical bear who usually left philosophy and theory to others. He enjoyed a physical challenge and his many scars held testament to his battles and bravery. But the light had made even his head consider and ponder what exactly it was that had entered Bear World without warning. The depth of his curiosity and interest in the discussions and theories had amazed him. Maybe there is more grey matter in this battered old bearskin than I realised, he chuckled to himself. Having completed the stave he searched the drawer for a new eye patch. The present one was worn and a bit scruffy. Can't go on parade with that he thought throwing it into the garbage can. He chose a brown eye patch and tried it on to gauge the effect. He adjusted it slightly, moving it to just below his left eyebrow ridge, so it fitted snugly. Satisfied that it looked good, he laid it carefully on the cabinet beside the stave. The only thing left to do was place alongside the other items the pair of silver backed brushes that he would use in the morning to make his fur ramrod straight and gleaming. Ablutions complete, Aiggrowgar strode eagerly to his camp bed, willing the morrow to arrive quickly. Enough time had been spent on talk and preparation, he was impatient for battle to commence.

The Grand Master, Winkington the 3rd, it really is a bit of a mouthful he thought ruefully, repeating it several times in his head. He was aware of how the senior and Trusted Bears saw him. Their friendships forged long before in shadowy periods half forgotten. Joint experiences and adventures shared, re-told on dark night-greys across time and space. A family honed by love not birth. Winkington was less sure how the adoption teddies viewed him. Oh they admired him, they sought to please him, they were happy when he spoke to them. He was the father-figure. But what did they think of him? What did they know of him? Not a lot, he mused. How could they. He glanced across at the shined anvil occupying one corner. Winkington the Blacksmith what would they think of him? That life had gone, now his was the responsibility of keeping Bear World running, of keeping it safe. Of making sure it would continue. It was his duty to decide how all this could be achieved. A lonely task and a heavy burden, but one he embraced with pride and devotion.

Winkington sat motionless in the comfort of his armchair, the only movement the raising of his paw to drink the hot sweet tea that had become a nightling ritual. This was his time to reflect on the passing dayling and to decide on the morrow. He sighed, a morrowmarch like the one approaching had not happened before and he wondered if his decisions would prove to be right. He had spoken to Rugle about his part in the battle and was troubled that once more he was asking his closest friend to risk his life for Bear World. Rugle fully recovered, was delighted to be involved and reassured the old bear that he would in no way be content to sit and watch. His flying skills were needed and if this truly was another dragon there was no choice but for him to be involved. Still Winkington was uneasy. He had faith in everything they had prepared and had no concerns as to the willingness and skill of all involved. But still he wondered what if Dooey's guess was wrong. What if something else entirely emerged from the light? What if……what if…..what if. Stop this Winkington, he scolded himself, defeat is not an option. We will win. Servo Veneflicus: Keep the Magic, I will not allow the castle to fall. He raised his now cool tea in a silent salute to the coat of arms above the mantle. Rising from his chair, he rubbed his massive paws over his head and muzzle, massaging the beige and greying fur and spoke firmly to himself. Get rid of this doubting face old bear, tomorrow you need a brave face and a strong voice to lead the bears to victory. He shook himself vigorously then strode towards the huge four poster bed.

The adoption bears were all sleeping soundly in their dormitories on their feather filled beds. They were tired from their exertions but excited by the coming event. Any danger to themselves had not occurred to them for they believed implicitly that the senior bears would never allow any harm to befall them. Denny dreamt of flying high in his glider, above the clouds in an azure blue sky, while Sarah and Ellie were snuggled up together snoring loudly. Jamie slept with a grin on his face for he had made a friend of his allotted partner.

Rugle tossed and turned upon the floor of the cave. First he was hot and drank from the stream, then he was cold and fired upon the boulders to warm himself. The melody of the flowing water soothed his thoughts, then it sounded too loud and annoyed him. What is the matter with you, he asked himself. The morrow will be busy, get some rest. He yawned and the rows of pointed teeth were exposed. He knew precisely what the matter was, but had not wanted to give the disturbing thoughts clarity. His task was to help his friends, he would defend them with his life, without query or concern. But another dragon!! According to Winkington and the others they were expecting a dragon to appear. I'm the last of my kind, he thought, or so I have always believed. If there is a chance another lives, am I to be its slayer? A dragon slayer, is that my fate Rugle worried. He left the cave and curled himself around the humped rock. If this light contains a dragon, then it is not as I and it cannot be good, he calculated. As he settled to sleep by the rolling waves Rugle knew that he would stand with his friends and fight, even if that meant he would be against his own breed.

Bearmont Guardian of the Castle

Chapter 12 THE BATTLE

Dawn

Thc Grand Master entered the kitchen expecting to be first on parade. He looked resplendent, his chain of office gleaming against the beige fur. The heavy burnished bronze chain supported a gold insignia of the coat of arms. Lovingly crafted by the bears who had lived in the Kingdom of Mercia when Wyrtgeorne (Vortigern) was King, the chain was beyond price and the most treasured possession in Bear World. Usually worn only at ceremonial occasions, Winkington had decided that this dayling called for the highest symbol in their world to be displayed for all to see.

Major Montgomery and Aiggrowgar had already arrived and were drinking their normal breakfast beverage; steaming hot tea sweetened with honey. Bearmont mused that it was as if a bell had rung, for all the senior bears had arrived within a few micros of each other. A full house; would there still be a full house at the end of the dayling? Bearmont pushed the thought away from the front of his mind and concentrated on Winkington, who having given everyone a chance to settle and take a few slurps of their chosen drink, was now about to speak.

"Bears, this dayling is one of the most important in our history. So much has been done in the past few daylings by way of preparation, not only with equipment, training and general battle readiness, but I have also read in your eyes the personal preparation that must take place.

I realise that some of you may have concerns about how well you will perform this day. Please be aware we are all as prepared and as ready as we can be. It is Bear Kingdom and all its inhabitants, wherever they dwell, that we are about to defend." With one pivot of his great head Winkington made eye contact with each bear present. Reassurance surged from him, entering deep within each one as he continued.

"We sit here this morning with some concern in our hearts, but we must remember our fore-bears and achieve this cycle what our fore-bears would expect of us. Good will triumph over bad. Your courage will bring us victory. I have no further instructions, we all know what we have to do. Go with our motto foremost in your minds, SERVO VENEFLICUS" The Grand Master rose from his seat, "Gentleb'rs to your posts. My heart is with you all."

Battle Stations

The battle plan began to take shape, the senior bears collected their radiophones. These gave each bear a direct link to Winkington. As the lines would remain open every bear would be aware of what commands were being given and what was happening in each area. The challenge would be to remember the strict discipline needed to use the phones correctly. Only one person could speak at a time and it was imperative to say 'over' when a message was complete. In this way a bear would know someone else could then speak. Coggrowgar, being a sea-captain had instructed the seniors in the procedure until he was satisfied they all understood.

William and Beggrowgar gathered all the castle bears into the Great Hall for the final briefing and for a few words of encouragement from Winkington.

"Good morning my brave cubs," he began standing tall, his strong shoulders carrying the weight of the chain. For many adoption bears this was the first time they had seen the fabled emblem and any apprehension they were feeling changed to awe and excitement. "You have all acquired the skills necessary for your designated task. Help your partner if necessary and work as a pairing, but remember, every reflector is vital to our success. If any bear is injured I would ask that you do not seek assistance until after the battle is completed. Harsh yes, but these are the realities of war. I know you understand, sacrifice and service is your whole way of life and not one of you would wish to endanger the outcome of this conflict." Winkington, with paws behind his back, smiled at the cubs before him.

"I want all the groups to be in place a few blinks before the middling. This time has been chosen as, when the sun reappears, it will be at its highest and give us the best opportunity for success." The Grand Master spread his long arms, embracing the teddy bears to him. "My dear cubs, may all that is good protect you and when in danger remember my thoughts and our motto will aid you."

The brave bears walked tall as they marched from the Hall. Watching them William curiously asked Aiggrowgar, who had joined them, "Why did you spend so much time teaching them how to drill, apart from the fact that they do look good and ordered now?"

“The concept of drill is to get a large number of bears to work together as a team. Drill is basically a team builder. It makes everyone equal, it builds pride and instils the discipline of doing as you are told immediately, without question, for the benefit and safety of all.” Aiggrowgar lowered his voice and as he too watched the bears, including Lady Linda, march proudly from the hall, he added gravely, “William my friend, learning to drill might just save some of our teddies their lives before this dayling is over.”

Everywhere on the crisped lawns and paths outside bears were engaged in preparing their stations. The courtyards within brimmed with bears organising equipment and hurrying to their allotted place. The castle wore the cacophony of sound that surrounded and engulfed it as if it were a shield. Coggrowgar’s starting cannon, used in pleasure times for sailing races, was heaved up to the ramparts of the central tower. It would be fired as the signal for the bears to turn their reflectors upside down and focus the light along the sights. Eaggrowgar had thought that there might be a need to turn the umbrellas down and back up again during the course of the battle, but it had been decided too many shots and commands could lead to confusion. One shot – one signal –one way, was the simplest solution.

Around the castle the forces were being deployed with the Grand Master bearing the Command Post, at the base of the centre tower. On the fore-shore, with a squadron of twenty bears each, Eaggrowgar and Duggrowsar were ensconced in the trenches dugout the previous dayling. Shaped in a crescent Duggrowsar placed equal numbers either side of her, allowing a 90 degree angle of reflection and a 45 degree angle of swing. Having identified Roger as a section leader, the large adoption bear was seated next to her. The radio phone was directly in front, built into the sand for protection and could easily be reached by her or Roger if the need arose. Roger had flown on an air-sea rescue helicopter with his last owner and would not panic in an emergency. Eaggrowgar had an identical set up to the west. The fore-shore position, away from the castle gave them unfettered access to the sky. An ideal position from which to refuel Rugle as he flew in from the sea.

Bearmont and Aiggrowgar were engaged with the Fire Chief in running hoses up to the top of the tower. Leighton had linked the trio of fire engine pumps together to increase the water pressure the Major had demanded. This would enable them to soak the light dragon on his first expected attack. Leighton had collected the honey from the kitchen and mixed it with just enough warm water to produce a wide spray. Aiggrowgar was fixing the system that would spray the feathers. Alarmingly it looked like a big dustbin, rolled onto its side and facing skywards. Gunpowder was at the base of the bin and feathers, from a quad of adoption bear beds, packed in on top. No-one knew whether the light-dragon would be translucent or be capable of making itself invisible. Covering it with feathers would make it identifiable.

Owing to the confined space on the stairways and on the ramparts it had been decided that the smaller bears would be better equipped to work at the tower. Now they were scampering up and down, carrying, fetching and setting up their reflectors ready to grab when needed. They had set up the flame shields along the length of the ramparts for protection if the dragon breathed flame. Buckets of water were placed next to each shelter. Leighton was relieved that the senior bears had not commandeered the largest fire engine, the turntable-ladder, circa 1964. He needed this for his fire-bears to use if the castle was burning.

Bearmont was marching stridently, checking angles, checking hoses, checking the feather gun, checking the reflectors, checking bears, in fact checking any object that stood, moved or made a sound within the tower. Time was running out and the middle-dayling was rapidly approaching.

William, Beggrowgar, Lexington & Coggrowgar moved out with their respective squadrons. Lexington had the balance of the small bears and he expected them to be nervous. He marched the bears out talking and assuring them but without treating them as youngsters. These were his bears, his big small bears, his little giants. He promised himself that the dayling would go well for his diminutive bears with enormous hearts. Lexington was an experienced battle bear and knew that his bears would grow in stature before the night-grey was upon them, but he was acutely aware that battles had a price and he hoped his losses would be nil. He arranged the bears so as to avoid cross-fire. The heat and light coming from a reflector at close range would be fatal for a small bear. His squadron was divided into a trio of sections, each with a different line of fire. In this way he decreased the danger as much as possible. His section leaders would have visual contact with Lexington at all times and all knew how to use the radiophone if he could not. The other senior bears were setting up their squadrons with just as much thought and concern for their teddy bears as had Lexington.

It was nearly middle-dayling. At the sound of the cannon all the bears would turn the reflectors up towards the light column. A calm had descended over the castle and the grounds. The only sound was the waves crashing along the shore. Some thought they could hear Rugle snorting, but it could have been the wind rustling through the dead and dying skeletal leaves that clung stubbornly to the orchard trees.

The radiophones rang, the septet of receivers were all picked up simultaneously. "This is the Grand Master, ten micros to the middling. Good luck to you all. Over"

The Major fired the cannon. It was exactly the middle-dayling.

The Assault

The micro the cannon sounded every bear, in one sweeping movement, up-turned their reflectors, lined up their sights and aimed at the light column. Instantly the light was reflected back upon itself *xv*-fold. The cubs stood firm controlling their reflectors, strong arm muscles pulsed but did not quiver. Not one beam of light wobbled as the column fought back, its energy bouncing to and fro. Suddenly the column's revolutions increased, they circled and spiralled as the light sensed it was attacking itself. Colours, intense in hue, shimmered within it, rainbows formed and dissipated. Lightning bolts, deep inside flashed from earth to sky. The illumination grew until it radiated as bright as the sun. Still the courageous bears held on, their eyes dazzled they squinted in the glare but dare not shut them. The senior bears roared encouragement as they too aimed their reflectors.

A voice bellowed from atop the tower; Aiggrowgar's.

"Hold fast comrades, hold fast, the thing is transforming. Be prepared."

The column narrowed, condensed, it leapt from the ground and tumbled from the sky. A gigantic globe formed spinning furiously, it exploded like a dying star. Heat and sparks spewed forth and this time the bears automatically lowered their reflectors, turned them down and used them as shields. When they looked up their breath stopped. Growing before them a phantom dragon was evolving in the space that the light had occupied. It duoed and trioed in size until the sky was obscured. As the wings unfurled the span dwarfed the castle quadrangle. The head was as long as the tower was tall. The teeth, all quad rows of them, were arrow sharp. Giant claws, curled as an eagle's when grabbing prey, gleamed crimson in the glow from the newly returned sun. Magnificent in its awfulness the fluorescent light dragon surveyed its foe. This was pure energy intent on the destruction of the castle.

Rugle had taken to the air well before the middling time to carry out a number of trial runs over the foreshore. This gave the bears a chance to practice fuelling Rugle before he climbed high above the castle in readiness for the battle. As the column transformed Rugle watched, with horrific fascination, the birth of his adversary. Startled by its size, thrice his own, he still breathed more easily at the realisation that this was not a fellow dragon, this was a phantom.

When Aiggrowgar had called out to the bears, Bearmont had busied himself reloading the starting cannon. Battle experience forewarned him that it might be needed again. As the light dragon prepared to attack Bearmont fired. The assembly, responding immediately, once more turned the reflectors, this time sighting the sun, ready to aid Rugle in his fight to remain the last dragon the world would ever see.

The phantom dropped its head and dived for the centre tower like a guided missile with a homing device. It swooped in from the sea using the speed it had gained from the dive, coming in low and parallel to the defending bears in the trenches. Bearmont, now directly facing him, raised the hose in readiness, he held steadfast, feet firmly on the ground, both paws wrapped securely around the nozzle, waiting for the foe to be in firing distance. Aiggrowgar, stationed by the feather cannon, had momentarily lost sight of the dragon being so low, but knew that until Bearmont opened up with the warm honey water he too was powerless to act. All the tower cubs were shielded behind the fire screens awaiting the next command. What they heard was not an order but an expletive.

"Great Grizzlies, it's pulled a feint on us!" Bearmont roared as the phantom veered to the left, well clear of the hose, rose upwards and came straight down firing a laser bolt behind one of the shields. It soared away from the tower towards the north, then circling round it started to make height, ready for a second attack. Hovering above the light dragon Rugle waited.

It had all happened so fast. Aiggrowgar was sprawled on his back, his language unrepeatable. The feather cannon had tripped him as he had tried to swing it round to follow the phantom's change of flight path. Bearmont sprang into the air, straddling the cannon and his friend in his haste to reach the shield that had taken a direct hit. A duo of bears lay so badly injured nothing could be done for them. He placed the damaged fire screen over the lifeless cubs. In the midst of battle it was a micro of quiet and thought, but no time for sorrow. They had to regroup and re-assess the situation.

Rugle noted the honey and feather plan had not succeeded at its first attempt. He desperately needed to distract the phantom from mounting a quick second attack until the bears had time to reorganise. From his height advantage he shot a searing flame of fire down towards the light dragon that was circling on its ascent. Phantom looked up as the fire shuddered through its luminescent body. It slowed and wobbled, pulling in the massive right wing to alter course.

Phantom now flew straight at the dragon. With the sun high in the sky Rugle had been partly fuelled by the rays, enough to race out across the sea. As he expected the phantom followed. Swerving, climbing and zig-zagging to avoid the laser bolts being fired at him Rugle lead the chase, always staying higher than his enemy. A 130 degree turn brought him onto a flight path that would take him over the south of the castle where Lexington waited with his squadron of small bears.

"Take aim my little giants, he's coming for our help." He shouted. As Rugle passed high above them, he felt the score of light-beams warm him. It was sufficient to enable him to outmanoeuvre the lightning bolt that struck the tinder dry trees in the orchard instead. Rugle headed back along the fore-shore but the light dragon doubled back towards the tower, this time approaching it from behind. On the ground the fire-bears raced to the orchard clanging the bell of the one remaining operational fire engine.

"Take cover AG Phantom to your rear." shouted Bearmont as Aiggrowgar struggled to his feet. He did not need to be told twice, a glance over his shoulder with his good eye, showed him Phantom closing in fast. The old warrior dived for cover close to the tower wall. As the light dragon swooped in Aiggrowgar saw it was so low and so close he could almost touch it. Instinctively he lunged out with his stave and swiped at the phantom. The stave passed through the open mouth bouncing along the opaque teeth.

"Blazes Alive," screamed Aiggrowgar, "the monster has taken the top off my stave, it's more like a spear now!"

"It won't surprise us a trio time AG. Next time we feather it," Bearmont yelled back.

The phantom swooped up to clear the flight path that Rugle was on. Rugle swerved, Phantom swung left. Rugle parried, Phantom countered. Both dragons were now locked in combat. Lightning bolts and fire rained down from the sky as the bears below watched in stunned silence at the aerial display. Rugle, although the smaller, was the more experienced having fought before in battle and in play. His heavy tail swung through the sky and caught the side of Phantom's head as he tried to avoid the body thrust. Slightly stunned Phantom broke away from the dog fight. The bears had found it difficult to keep the reflectors on Rugle but now, for a few micros, he was on his own. A flood of light hit him and he took the chance of opening his scales a fraction to take onboard more of the heat coming from below. The Grand Master, watching the dragons battle, picked up the radiophone, waited for the septet of lights on the panel to blink on and roared at his comrades.

"Bears, the phantom is sapping vast amounts of energy and heat from Rugle whenever it gets close to him. We must keep the light aimed on Rugle for as long as possible. Good luck. Over"

Both dragons were trying to get the height advantage. Rugle already had the advantage of the sun behind him, so gaining fuel and making it difficult for the phantom to see him clearly. During the ascent the cubs had managed to keep most of their reflectors on Rugle following the prompting from the senior bears after the Grand Master's call.

Rugle, now fully recharged, gained the height needed to swoop down and fly over the tower. He needed the speed a high dive would give him to keep Phantom at bay. He turned 180 degrees and headed for the tower where the bears were now re-organised and ready. As he crossed the light dragon's path Rugle took the full force of the lightning bolt aimed at him. It hit the leathery part of his wing and a hole the size of a barrel opened. It was not a major injury but enough to make him swerve off course. The swerve saved him for as a second laser bolt gushed from Phantom's open jaws, it overshot Rugle but made a direct hit on the west wall of the castle.

"Look out my Salties," Coggrowgar cried as masonry, glass and timber thundered down upon the cubs. He was pinned beneath a heavy oak beam and knew immediately his leg was broken. Several of the adoption bears started to lay down their reflectors and gallop to his aid. He halted them in their tracks.

"Stay at your posts, stay at your positions. Remember what the Grand Master said, no aid for the injured," Coggrowgar roared at the top of his voice. "Reflectors on Rugle, you must help him. Jamie you are section leader, bear the phone. Inform Winkington everything here is still under control." Coggrowgar may have been unable to move, but he was still very much in command.

Winkington, having taken young Jamie's call, spoke directly to Bearmont. "Rugle's coming in, are you ready? Over," he yelled.

"Aye aye, everything's ready," the Major responded, forgetting the 'over' as he watched Rugle approaching at high speed with the phantom chasing only a league behind.

Rugle having corrected his course was coming in from the sea. As he flew over William's squadron the large cubs refuelled him mid-flight and cheered him on his way.

Bearmont, once more posed with the hose, bellowed hoarsely at Aiggrowgar, "They're coming, it's happening…steady…steady."

The Grand Master was watching intently every move Rugle was making. In his head he was riding on the dragon's back as he had done many times over the years. Exhilarated, but desperately concerned for Rugle's safety, he was unknowingly shouting up at his great friend encouraging him on. With the phantom close on his tail Rugle knew he needed speed. He must not let Phantom catch up or even get too close. He had no desire for another hit from a lightning bolt. Wings tucked in tight, tail straight, he increased to the limit his speed. The wind created flattened his ears and tightened his jaw. Phantom was closing but not quickly enough.

Bearmont could now see Rugle was going to skim in just over their heads. He was giving his friends the best chance they had of success. Phantom was so intent on catching the dragon nothing else mattered. It did not see the danger it was heading towards as it closed in on its prey, claws swinging round to the front in readiness.

Aiggrowgar bristled with excitement, the tension at the top of the tower mounted. His fur blew backwards as the rush of air forced down by Rugle's wings swept over him, "Come on, come on you sack of nothingness," he screamed as the light dragon entered the range of fire.

WHOOOSH the honey water sprayed over Phantom, just as his claws reached forward. BANG the dustbin cannon exploded, feathers filled the air and as the smoke cleared the bears saw the phantom was now covered on one complete side with white feathers.

Time stood still as the light dragon stopped dead, not sure of what had happened or what to do. Suddenly it spun round to fly south and for the first time, on its light side, the burning golden orb heart of the vulnerable creature was visible within its chest.

Now it was Rugle's turn to give chase. Again both dragons started the deadly dance of circling to gain height. Bearmont instructed the remaining eighteen bears to clear the feather cannon out of the way. Aiggrowgar was busy moving the starting cannon into position then he loaded it with the broken pointed stave.

"If it's got a heart we can kill it. We'll harpoon the wretched thing if we have to. Over," he explained to Winkington and the senior bears via the radiophone.

"What do you think Dooey?" asked Winkington. "Should we try a shot? Over"

"Yes, it has to be a vulnerable part of him. It's beating. Over"

Eaggrowgar joined in, "There must be some substance to the heart, the rest is just light. Over."

"Good, good we have a plan." Winkington looked up at the duo of dragons, swirling and duelling in the air above. "We are fuelling Rugle as much as we can, but it doesn't stop the phantom. Let's see if we can do that. Bearmont, I want one shot on the cannon. When the rest of you hear it, get your bears to down their reflectors from Rugle, count to ten and bring them back up onto the phantom. I repeat onto the phantom. I hope this will overload him enough to give Rugle the advantage. I only hope that he will see what we are up to. Over and out".

After Aiggrowgar removed his spear the Major fired the cannon. Like clockwork the bears counted down – ten, nine; the voices rose, eight, seven; the excited bears grew louder, six, five; it was a crescendo, four; the voices were deafening, three. Rugle's sharp ears picked up the count, he swerved away then hovered, waiting for something to happen. No light was shining upwards; he heard the count of two, what next? The bears were going to attack Phantom! This was going to be a joint attack. This was going to be a death blow. Rugle began his plunge towards the phantom as the light beams from all the bears hit it at the same time. Sparks radiated from the light side of the phantom and it did not turn to meet Rugle's attack. He did have the advantage. The fire in his belly grew, it swelled, it zoomed up into his chest as he closed on his foe. Wings angled back, mouth opening, the fire spurted into his throat filling his mouth and his nostrils, preventing him from breathing, the gagging reflex propelled the flames outward directly onto the shocked Phantom.

The feathers caught light long enough to cause burns to the luminescent wing and the neck and shoulder on one side. The light dragon emitted a terrible high pitched screech of anger and pain. It shocked all who heard, for in its vulnerability this was becoming a creature and not just light. The phantom recovered some of its balance and dived away from Rugle. For a final time it headed for the castle determined to inflict whatever damage it could still do.

Aiggrowgar had reloaded the cannon complete with his damaged stave. With the aid of a quartet of the cubs he bear-handled the cannon over to the south side of the castle tower. He was gambling that the phantom would again come in from over the sea. The warrior in him knew most things are creatures of habit. When hurt, instinct dominates and he guessed Phantom would follow its same line of attack as before.

Winkington's mind was racing, he was missing something. The light shock had worked. Rugle's attack had worked. He thought back over the past dayling, what had been said? The light had taken on Rugle's shape. It had wanted a heart to be able to fight. It had attacked the tower as the heart of the castle. It had a heartbeat…..as did the tower! That was it, the tower had a heartbeat. Winkington could see the phantom flying towards the castle, swooping in from the sea. A chilling spectacle, the wings were out of sync. The damaged wing, smouldering from the flames, flapped loosely, the other had to compensate continuously to keep the creature on its chosen trajectory. Rugle was approaching from the north-east allowing William, Beggrowgar and the fore-shore bears to refuel him as he passed.

Winkington could hear the ticking of the clock. In his haste he stumbled up the two steps to the open door of the rest room. He could see the clock on the wall with its swinging pendulum, grabbing the chain of office from around his neck he swung it round his head and let loose all in one sling shot. The chain whirled through the air, entangled the pendulum and the clock stopped. Outside the phantom kept coming but there was a difference in its movement. The mouth stayed shut, the wings slowed, the intent and consciousness was gone. It looked as if it was going to crash into the tower. The phantom lifted its head but as it tried to swerve away from the tower it exposed its underside. Aiggrowgar, ready as ever, waited a micro, took aim and pulled the trigger. The pointed stave shot from the cannon finding its target; the glowing orb inside the light dragon. Its single heart, already attacked, stopped completely. Phantom spun over and crashed to the ground. Rugle followed it down in a vertical dive as the bears below cheered, waved their reflectors and danced up and down. When Rugle landed all that remained of his opponent was thousands of minute shiny spheres. They rolled across the fore-shore and as the astonished bears watched the twinkling spheres dissolved into the sea.

Chapter 13 AFTERMATH

Jamie, Denny and Ollie built the funeral pyre high. Tears mingled with sweat and dark stains tram-lined their face fur. Other cubs had chopped and hauled the wood from the forest to the High Point that soared vertically above the fore-shore. Lenny, the cheeky adoption bear who had told his last-life story to William such a short time ago and Percy, a castle bear who had worked in the kitchens for a demi-million cycles, had been in the centre tower squadron when the lightning bolts had struck. This duo of dead bears now rested in open wicker baskets, skilfully crafted by Woodrow and his team. The girl cubs, organised by Ellie, covered them in white cyclamen and winter aconite flowers. Their pillows were myriad shades of lilac heather. Duggrowsar, sorrowing at her inability to help the small cubs, dressed the finished pyre with sweet-smelling herbs and spices.

All was ready as the newly awakened sun reached its zenith. The entire population lined up in rows, in their squadrons, behind Winkington. The Grand Master, again wearing the great chain of office, stood in front of the caskets.

"Let us pay honour." His voice travelled across the heads of the assembled company and they bowed. Winkington turning his back picked up the hawsers one in each paw and pulled his beloved cubs to their final departure place. He passed between the timber ramps on the pyre and climbing the side he heaved the wicker baskets carefully into place on the flat top.

The bears had marched solemnly to the beat of Eaggrowgar's drum. Aiggrowgar wore a scarlet eye patch and carried a new stave bearing a pair of leafy shoots, symbolising the little cubs transition to a new world. Coggrowgar had hopped along on his crutches, his massive arms supporting his weight allowed him to keep pace.

Rugle was waiting at the top of the High Point. To him fell the duty of lighting the pyre. With the Grand Master now in place, Rugle crouched low, his elongated neck stretching along the ground and with a quartet of gentle puffs ablazed the cedar and pine woods. The bears now formed a circle. The females sang in their high falsetto voices joyous songs to celebrate the numerous lives of Lenny and Percy. The males hummed the accompaniment with their resonating, rolling base tones. They watched the fire sparks, bright and as gay as fireworks ascending to the sky and the stars above.

Going back they gambolled and tumbled their way to the kitchen, gleefully sharing tales about the departed bears. They ate the prepared hot porridge and sweet-meat berries and stood for the Toast intoned by Winkington.

"We give thanks to the Universe for lending us our brave little bears, whose friendship we will celebrate but greatly miss. May good speed and prosperity go with them across time and space."

The senior bears, lead by the Grand Master, then left the cubs still eating, to return to the library and plan the repair of the castle.

Chapter 14 NEW BEGINNINGS

Rebuilding the castle was a hectic, noisy task, undertaken with great enthusiasm by all the bears. Lexington arranged for a trio of Egyptian stone-masons to arrive. They cut and shaped the massive boulders to fit exactly the spaces between the damaged masonry and to fashion the new rows required to repair the damaged tower. Toomey, the museum bear from Cairo, had taken advantage of the stone-masons visit and travelled with them to hear the tale of the light-dragon and the battle. The Grand Master welcomed them all warmly and was delighted to show Toomey the castle and relate some historic tales.

Woodrow and his team of workshop bears hammered, chiselled and felled heavy branches from the giant oaks to replace broken beams. Doors and window frames were mended and a trio of adoption bears needed new beds. Their old ones were destroyed when a laser beam had entered through the shattered window. The rest of the senior bears organised work parties to replant the orchards and reseed the scorched lawns and flower beds. The kitchen bears, always busy during normal times, now found meal-times occurring non-stop throughout the cycle as hungry bears poured in, conveyor belt fashion, to consume vast bowls of honey porridge and massive plates of fish stew. Fresh fruit, in short supply with the destruction of the orchards, was mysteriously replaced with baked apples and banana fritters gathered by Rugle on frequent trips to man-world during the night-dark. In spite of all the hard work a not inconsiderable number of bears found their waist-lines speedily expanding.

Duggrowsar, aided by several girl adoption bears, applied her poultices and bandaged bruised heads and limbs. After plastering Coggrowgar's leg she had ordered him to rest, only to watch him on the coming morrows speeding along on his crutches that Woodrow had made specifically for him.

"Don't you worry Dooey, I still have my good leg to heave along on, 'tis only the gammy one that got broken!" the old sea-captain explained cheerfully when Duggrowsar admonished him for not resting. "I'll be dancing a hornpipe again for the young salties before the moon is new."

Replacing the window in the West Wing with new toffee-scented glass proved problematic. When the castle was built it had been the most popular glass in Bear World. Centuries later_the art of scenting glass had long been forgotten. William, searching through the volumes of invoices and accounts, eventually discovered one remaining family in Arabia who could possibly be of help. So it was a twice-octet of morrows later that the new glass arrived by sea. The trading boat sailed into the bay to cheers and much flag waving. Rugle circled above, gently blowing warm air into the billowing sails to hasten the arrival and guide the foreign ship away from the hidden rocks. Coggrowgar, refusing to be thwarted by such a trifling handicap as a broken leg, had clambered aboard his beloved dingy and instructed Jamie – a constant companion since the accident - to sail out to greet the Arabian bears and to act as a pilot boat escorting them into the bay. When the glass was unloaded and being carried to the castle there was much excitement and sniffing among the adoption bears, especially when they realised that this time the scent was not caramel but fudge. Overseen by Lexington, the window was hoisted aloft and placed securely in position as all the castle bears danced, sang and tumbled around on the newly growing lawns. The fitting of the window was the final repair of the damage sustained by the castle during the battle. Celebrations were in order.

The Debrief

Once more the senior bears sat around the crystal table in the Spell-room. Winkington had ordered a review of all the events leading up to the battle and its conclusion.

"My friends, we have triumphed over the light and its transformation into the light dragon. For that success, again I thank you, but that success has also cost us dearly in the lives of our brave cubs. We must examine everything we did, everything we learnt and everything we shared. Can we learn anything for the future if another threat comes upon us?"

"I believe the actual battle went well," said Bearmont. "We were well prepared, well equipped and our bears well trained."

"I think so too," agreed Aiggrowgar. "Considering we did not know exactly who or what our assailant was we did extremely well. The reflectors EG devised were brilliant."

"Don't get me wrong," Winkington smiled, "yes, we did remarkably well, but I want the whole episode written up and recorded for the future. There is so much we have learnt but also some things we would do differently or even not at all."

Bearmont growled, "We know, we know, the fire engine escapade!!" All the bears laughed and Aiggrowgar slapped his friend on the back with a resounding thud.

“Ah not to worry if the others think we are a pair of old pandas, it was fun and exciting my Old Pup wasn’t it.”

William offered to undertake the task of recording the whole event and then storing it in the library. “It won’t be an onerous task as Beggrowgar and I have already written copious notes of events as they have taken place; Rugle’s flight, the glider attack, the trip to Egypt, all the information gathered and we can add the notes EG and Dooey used....”

“Yep, we’ve got the picture and I think you’ve got the job.” Coggrowgar interrupted guffawing loudly.

Winkington joined in the laughter, “Good, good that’s sorted then. One more thing my friends, I propose that we have a Thank You Ceremony beside the Wisdom Tree.”

Bearmont and Aiggrowgar suddenly sat up very straight, nudging each other under the table, as they remembered their conversation from when they devised the fire engine plan. Plan B had been a brilliant idea, even if it had not been successful.

The Grand Master continued, “The glider plan was excellent, even though it did not have the expected outcome.....”

The Major puffed out his chest and Aiggrowgar adjusted his eye patch, already planning his reluctant acceptance to this great honour about to be bestowed.

".......I therefore recommend that for courage and braveness above what is expected of normal duties, Denny our little glider pilot is awarded this honour."

All the bears shouted agreement and clapped their approval and no bear clapped harder than Major Montgomery and Aiggrowgar.

The Ceremony

None of the adoption bears living at the castle had witnessed a Thank You Ceremony before. It was such a rare occasion some imagined it was just legend, tales from bear history of long ago. Honoured bear exploits were handed down from generation to generation, their tales of bravery and sacrifice enthralling all who heard. Thus the excitement of all the castle bears was immense, not only would they partake in the ceremony but they actually knew the recipient. For the quadful of morrows, while everything was being prepared, Denny was the most popular bear at the castle and even gave autograph sessions and retellings of 'The Great Glider Gravitation' episode immediately after breakfast in the castle kitchen.

The morrowmarch arrived and all was ready. Picnic rugs and deckchairs had been laid out on the newly growing lawns in front of the Wisdom Tree. Rainbow coloured sparkling lights adorned the branches. Flags from all regions of Bear World fluttered in the soft breeze from a semi-circle of redwood poles. The dozen giant carvings of the warrior bears had been hauled along rollers and placed in an opposite semi-circle, in front of the Wisdom Tree, so that the arena was now marked out. The gold-leafed ornate chairs stood glittering in the early sun. They formed their own row in front of the warrior bear carvings. Each senior bear had his own chair and carved into the screen backs was the name and lineage of each one. On the top of the Grand Master's chair, encrusted with diamond dust, was a replica of the coat of arms.

The bugles started playing a rousing march by J.P.Sousa to announce the beginning of the ceremony. At once the castle bears, who had been tumbling and rolling down the grassy banks or playing chase with friends scrambled for their seats. They brushed themselves free of leaves and twigs, vigorously shook their fur and clapped along to the music while awaiting the arrival of the senior bears. The Grand Master led the parade, wearing the golden-brown Robe of Office with its silk scarlet lining and the chain once more around his neck he marched through the flagpoles, through the middle of the arena and stopped in front of his throne. The other senior bears marched behind until all had taken their places. Coggrowgar, the last in the line, placed his crutches at the side of his chair, then sat with his plastered leg stuck straight out in front. Aiggrowgar wore a white eye-patch while Duggrowsar had pinned a yellow and white corsage of tiny flowers near her left ear. Winkington stood, took a duo of steps forwards and said,

"Welcome everybear. This dayling we are here to give our thanks and to recognise the valour of one of our adoption bears. I do not need to tell you how special this occasion is. Only the very bravest of bears can be awarded a Thank You Ceremony. Only a bear prepared to risk and lay down his life for Bear World can be honoured in this way. It gives me and all the senior bears here immense pleasure and great pride to be able to conduct this ceremony here beside the Wisdom Tree."

Winkington sat down. The cubs wondered what was to happen next, for as they turned and twisted, craned their necks and asked their neighbours, all were aware that one bear was missing. Where was the recipient? The bugles sounded a fanfare and from above the arena a great roar was heard. Heads turned skywards and circling slowly was Rugle. Accompanied by gasps from the bears, Rugle spiralled downwards until finally, when level with the top of the Wisdom Tree, the bears could see Denny sitting astride Rugle's shoulders waving at them. The bears jumped up and began shouting, cheering, laughing and waving back at their overjoyed friend. Rugle did a final flypast and landed just beyond the flagpoles. When Denny had disembarked and strutted towards the Wisdom

Tree Rugle adopted a sphinx position with his neck raised just high enough to watch the rest of the proceedings.

Winkington opened his arms and engulfed the little bear in one of his famous bear-hugs. Upon release Denny gasping for air turned and grinned and waved at all his comrades. With his arm around Denny's shoulder Winkington spoke once more to the gathered assembly.

"My friends, it is the duty of each senior bear to bestow upon the recipient a gift of their own choosing. Rugle our great friend wanted to be part of that and he chose, as you saw, to fly Denny here. No bear, apart from me, has ever ridden on Rugle's back. It is the most prized gift he could offer." The bears clapped and cheered again. Winkington then looked left then right along the row of chairs and extended his free paw towards William. "So, I invite you all in turn to give your gifts and explain your choice."

Denny stepped forward as William approached. "Glass is my gift to you, please accept this snow globe containing a miniature of Wynghorran castle. It is the only one of its kind. I hope it will always remind you of happy times here."

"Thank you," said Denny giving the globe a hefty shake and watching the snow fall around the castle.

Bearmont stood before Denny and saluted him. "My gift is a silver replica of the keys of the castle. You are now a freebear of Wynghorran and it will always be your home."

"Wow, ta very much."

Aiggrowgar harrumphed and cleared his throat. "I whittled this from the remains of the stave that killed the phantom. I want it to always remind you of your bravery young cub," he said as he handed him a wooden model of the glider.

"Brilliant." Denny zoomed the glider through the air before putting it on the small ebony table next to him alongside the other gifts.

"This book contains the tales of all the other bears who have received a Thank You Ceremony. One day your name will be in a book just like it," said Beggrowgar smiling.

"D'ya really think so!"

Next Coggrowgar lumbered forward on one crutch holding a cap in the other paw. "This is a sea-captain's hat. Wear it whenever you want to sail with me and I will be proud to crew for you."

Even Denny realised what an honour and a sacrifice this was being offered to him by the sailor. "Thank you very much Captain," he said shyly putting the cap on his head.

Skipping from her chair, Duggrowsar gave Denny a peck on each side of his muzzle and gave him an exquisite purple coloured crystal glass bottle. "I want you to have these spices. Wherever you are, however you feel, just smell them and you will remember Wynghorran and that we are always your friends and always here for you."

"That's pretty." He carefully put the bottle on top of the book.

Eaggrowgar withdrew from the bamboo tube the drawing he was carrying and showed Denny the diagram. "This is the original diagram I drew of the reflectors. I hope you will think it a worthy gift. I want you to remember the big part you played in our battle to defeat the light dragon."

"Corr, thanks mate," growled Denny, forgetting that he was addressing a Trusted Bear. Such was the occasion that all the bears laughed including the senior ones and even Winkington himself.

"Mine is the last personal gift, my little friend," Lexington began. "I discovered from your friends that you enjoy puzzles, so I have made you this wooden pyramid. It comes to pieces and hopefully you will enjoy trying to assemble it again. Each piece is made from different woods in our orchards and forest. Like the others I want to remind you of your time here."

"Perfect. Thank you. Thank you all, they're all brilliant."

Winkington stood opposite the little bear but turned his head towards the cubs.

"My gift is the medal awarded to those honoured with a Thank You Ceremony." Winkington opened the intricately carved box on the table and held up the medal for all to see. Made from a tiny piece of the sword carried into battle by Richard the Lionheart, the metal now bore the insignia of Bear World's coat of arms. Underneath was the motto 'Servio Veneflicus'. The ribbon was woven from silk and spider's thread and coated with star-dust collected when the moon was new. The arena was still, no sound, no movement as the Grand Master placed the ribbon over Denny's head and the medal glistened in the rays from the sun. From the top of the central tower the cannon fired. Leighton had been waiting for this moment to send his salute. The bears stampeded around the arena and towards Denny. They cheered, they stamped, they sang, they climbed on each other's shoulders and marched up and down. They congratulated each other and Denny. They thumped their nearest neighbour with chest greetings and rolled higgley-piggley as far as they could. Rugle sent a jet of fire so high into the sky some thought it would reach the sun. Throughout this celebration Denny stood next to the Grand Master holding his paw and wept. Never had he been so happy or so overwhelmed. Not one bear there could remember a better or more exciting dayling in all the history of Wynghorran Castle.

Chapter 15 FLYPASS

Winkington was satisfied as he walked down the path from the castle to the fore-shore. Everything appeared normal again. Code Indigo had been downgraded to the normal Code Pearl. The castle bears were back to their usual duties and the adoption bears were playing and recuperating from all the recent happenings. Each one he saw wanted to chat and recount their part in the battle or tell how exciting it was to have taken part in the Thank You Ceremony. He noted that none mentioned the funeral and this pleased him. It meant that like him, they missed but accepted the loss of their friends. Although sad to part with comrades bears lives were made up of service and duties in man-world, this was usually a solitary task and meeting with friends was infrequent. Death was also just a doorway, no bear knew what was on the other side but all believed it lead to another adventure. He had passed the Major near the top of the path; Bearmont was again walking the castle and its grounds, listening to its sighs and creaks.

As Winkington thumped along the soft sand he saw Rugle leap down from his rock and stand alert ready to welcome him. Contentment swam through the Grand Master's chest and became a smile as it exited his body. He waved to his closest friend who was already unfurling one wing to wrap around him in greeting. Rugle was the only creature who, in size and intimacy of long friendship, could envelop Winkington and make him feel safe.

"It's good to see you Old Bear," Rugle said as they stepped apart. "Good to see you without having to discuss problems."

Winkington nodded agreement. "You too my friend, you too." They sat side by side, Rugle sprawled along the sand while the Grand Master sat with his back resting against the rock. Rugle laid one wing over the boulder shielding the beige coloured bear from the high sun for it was hot and even bears can burn.

"Everything back to normal up there?" Rugle asked indicating towards the castle with a glance of his massive head.

"Yes, at last I believe it is. For the first time in many daylings I felt contentment coming down here. The danger to Bear World is past, for the present."

The grimbled dragon raised one eyebrow, "For the present?"

“Yes for the present. Remember the light came here but it was made up of all the ills in man-world. We haven’t changed those ills and so I have given it a lot of thought.”

“But you look much more relaxed Old Bear. You’re not still worrying are you?”

“No.” Winkington shifted about trying to fit his contours into the rock and wriggling deeper into the sand, his ample rump making a matching indentation for comfort. “I spent the past night-dark thinking it through and I’ve come to a conclusion.”

Winkington’s thoughts drifted back to his deliberations of the past sleep cycle. He had been saddened and dismayed at how much and how quickly man-world had changed. He had listened to the adoption bears stories retold to him by William and Beggrowgar. He had studied the camera obscura and watched for himself. He had come to the conclusion that scores of humans are full of craving. They are occupied with envy, jealousy, mistrust and fear. These were the elements that created the light. This was the custard waiting to escape and fall on them. This was the substance of the light-dragon. The humans were always hurrying to fill the craving, to always buy more and more but it did not make them content. Always they scurry with no time to eat, they graze all day; while walking, while travelling, while working, while watching the screens. They build quick eating shops. They talk always, but with devices; at home, at work, in the street, in cars, on buses. They talk with the world and believe this is friendship.

They talk or finger talk about the craving and when they have the craving they change and update the craving. They take to special shops the many of the same things. They take the never used things and exchange or buy more never to be used things. Children have their own special shops of craving things. They watch the screens and are told what to crave. Saddest of all they crave not just possessions but people. They crave different people and break families. They work so hard to buy the cravings and are still not satisfied.

Others who cannot or will not work also crave, they too watch the screens and they talk with the devices about how unhappy they are. Worst of all are the angry ones. They drink and fall down a lot. They crave very bad things that they ingest by vile means. They are violent, they shout and fight and steal. Too many of these are very young in man-years, still children. They crave but have no hope. For many humans man-world has become an unhappy place.

“So, what is your conclusion?” asked Rugle as he tore into quarters the meat he had just flame grilled on the sand.

Winkington held the meat in both paws and tore off a big chunk with his jagged sharp teeth. It was hot and he gulped in air and stuck out his tongue.

“Most of man-world is still good but many are caught up with the buying and having. They have forgotten how to enjoy simple pleasures. So we will have to remind them.” He tentatively tried the meat again.

“How will we do that?”

“We’ll remind them of the goodness of bears and aim for every adoption bear to be loved and born, so that they can help their owners. Many have forgotten the magic and pleasure of having one special bear. A special bear they can tell their secrets and fears and hopes to. A special bear for life. That’s my aim.” Winkington leaned back against the rock once more and waited for the next course, the long conger eel, to be cooked.

“Great idea Old Bear, I like it, but still not sure how you’re going to achieve it.”

“We’ll have to compete with whatever it is children now want, if that means taking on Time Lords and Boy Wizards, Star Troopers and Droids and other such things then so be it.”

Rugle threw back his head and roared a laugh. "Ah ha, another battle eh, but a fun one. Good, wouldn't want things to get too boring around here."

"It won't. I'm even thinking of getting some of the senior bears to go back out to man-world and work alongside man once again. See what's happening, new discoveries, new beginnings here and out there. Get an overview, we've lost touch a bit. William and BG are already working on some new spells and a trio of cubs are ready to leave on the morrowmarch. It's all going to happen I'm sure of it."

Winkington stood, vigorously shook the sand and food crumbs from his fur and rubbed his back against Rugle's hind leg in an affectionate gesture of departure. "Great lunch as usual my fine friend. Thank you."

"Talking of overviews, how about a quick fly around the estate, help me stretch my wings?" Rugle unfurled his wings and arced them above his head sending the blood to course to every edge and point in readiness for flight.

"O.K. trusted steed, let's go. We still have time for fun." The Grand Master hurled himself onto Rugle's neck and slid backwards until his rump rested between the bony shoulder blades. With one paw each side of a pair of the serrated scales Rugle began his flight run.

High above the castle they could see the cubs playing below and hear their laughter. Rugle swooped past Bearmont, now patrolling at the top of the tower.

"Good morning to the pair of you," he shouted merrily.

Just before they crashed into the library window Rugle turned 90 degrees towards the sea. Winkington glimpsed William busy inside searching for a spell.

Spells that had been passed down over many centuries were guarded by William: the Keeper of Spells. It was his task to protect them and no other bear was able to access the spell books. William's magic was strong and any intruder would be turned into everlasting dust that would be cast out through the tiny cracks in the castle walls and float throughout the universe for eternity. Spells could only be used for good deeds and were used by the adoption bears when their owners needed help. The bears would call to the Grand Master or William and they would always hear them, wherever the bears were kept.

William would choose a spell and send to the teddy bears to help them with their bear duties. Choosing a spell was a solemn, important occasion. William would summon Beggrowgar to help. The rituals had to be carried out in the correct order or the spell would not work. The pair of bears was now engrossed in this very process. William was walking up and down the rows of books. He walked slowly, searching, reading the ancient titles. There were many rows of books and sometimes he would walk back and forth, chanting the magic words known only to him, for a twelfth of the dayling. He stopped, one book began to shine, a rainbow cascaded from the book to the Keeper's paw. He then knew this was the book he needed. Beggrowgar carefully took the book from the shelf and placed it on the crystal table. The secret ritual for choosing the specific spell then began.

As Rugle flew low over the sea Winkington could see Coggrowgar in his dingy with an excited Jamie and Denny. Denny was wearing his sea-captain's hat which he took off and waved to the duo above. Coggrowgar was pulling in the gib showing the cubs how to tack. On his way back to the fore-shore Rugle circled the main gate-way where Aiggrowgar was standing.

An adoption bear was skipping along the cobbles towards the gate where the old warrior waited beneath the wrought iron portcullis.

"Hello my little cub, come on this way," he hollered while beckoning with his left arm. "Come on in."

The little bear ran towards him, gave him a quick hug and then looked up shyly, wondering if the hug had been in order.

Aiggrowgar laughed, "Well that's a mighty fine greeting, we've been expecting you. Have you been here before?"

"No, this is the first time."

Moving his stave to the other paw Aiggrowgar put his free arm around the cub's shoulder and moved into the courtyard.

"Goodness me, then we have got a lot to show you, but there's plenty of time. I'll show you where you are going to stay and introduce you to the other adoption bears. You'll soon make friends." Aiggrowgar let out a deep growl and slapped himself on the head. The startled bear looked up at him.

"Introduce you! Huh a fine host I am. Haven't introduced myself have I. Getting old and forgetful, that's me." He twisted round to face the newcomer and smiled, "I'm Aiggrowgar a Trusted Bear. And you?"

"I'm Susan," was the proud reply.

"Well I welcome you little girlie," said Aiggrowgar bowing and then he placed his paw once more upon her shoulder and led her towards the west wing.

"You're going to love it here at Wynghorran Castle Susan, living here is magic."

****